COMMITTED

Delta Family Romances #3

CAMI CHECKETTS

COPYRIGHT

Committed: Delta Family Romances #3

Copyright © 2022 by Cami Checketts

All rights reserved.

No part of this book may be reproduced in any form or by any electronic or mechanical means, including information storage and retrieval systems, without written permission from the author, except for the use of brief quotations in a book review.

FREE BOOK

Receive a free copy of *Seeking Mr. Debonair: The Jane Austen Pact* by clicking here and signing up for Cami's newsletter.

CHAPTER ONE

Alivia Delta strode across the dirt path and to the future front door of one of her custom-built homes under construction. A light summer breeze kissed her face, and she felt on top of the world. The construction world, at least. Her reputation had spread over the past ten years, and she now had new builds underway in several towns throughout Colorado, besides all the jobs in her home base of Summit Valley. Her homes were beautiful, reasonably priced, well-built, and she prided herself on giving the client exactly what they wanted. It was exhausting at times, but she had the time.

She leaped onto the porch—the steps hadn't been poured yet—and eased into the nine-foot double archway where the door would be installed later today.

Building and designing homes was her passion, and she couldn't care less that she was a woman in a man's world. She'd never connected with female friends besides her sisters and loved being around men and teasing and laughing with them. She could also claim she worked as hard and had as much knowledge as any man in the industry. Well, any man besides ...

She cleared the entryway and there he was. Klein Vance. In all his manly glory. He was the most beautiful male she'd ever encountered, and she'd encountered a lot of them in her line of work. She also had close relationships with her brother and male cousins and had met impressive football players, lacrosse players, military men, and cowboys through those relationships.

No man could ever affect her or draw her in like Klein. He was only a few inches taller than her five-eleven but made her feel small and dainty because of his broad shoulders and well-built body. She could swear his muscles had muscles, and the man could wear a tool belt like nobody's business.

Her sister Jessie called him the "suave, sexy stud." Alivia tried very hard not to think of those words when he met her gaze. She loved his dark wavy hair, expressive green eyes, tanned skin, short facial hair, and even features. Handsome wasn't enough to describe Klein, but it was his work ethic, fairness with their employees, loyalty to her, his sister, and his grandmother, patience, faith, kindness, and irresistible grin that really drew her in. She'd known him all her life, but hadn't fully appreciated all his great qualities until they'd started working together. He was thirty, the same age as her older brother Colton. Three years older than her. About the perfect span of age, if you asked her.

He turned, and even as the impact of those green eyes hit her, she steeled herself and forced her expression into neutral. It was rough, but no way, no how was she revealing to this beautiful man, or anyone else, that the tomboy Alivia Delta was head over heels for her general manager.

Alivia didn't know the meaning of makeup, a hairstyle other than her long blonde hair in a ponytail, or work pants or boots that didn't come from the men's section of Cal Ranch. She wore a different high-quality Delta Builders T-shirt to work each day paired with one of her pairs of cargo pants, with the secret pocket that contained a thin knife nobody but her would ever find. Of course she had a pocketknife as well. The secret knife was courtesy of her Papa and only for emergencies.

Every guy treated her as his buddy and she'd never kissed a boy or man. She wasn't a good fit for the "suave, sexy stud" and she knew it. Besides that, her business came first. She was not about to mess up the incredible working relationship she and Klein had going.

"Ali," he said, that slow grin growing on his face.

Alivia's legs went gooey. How could she be so tough around everyone, trained by her Papa to fight like a military weapon as part of the Delta Protection Detail, and teased by her two younger sisters that she didn't even know what female emotion was, but want to bat her eyelashes and lick her lips when she came face to face with the man who needed to be off limits to her? She couldn't imagine what a mess a romantic entanglement would be with her top employee slash business partner. The entire world, or at least all of Summit Valley, would laugh to think Alivia had any hope of Klein Vance returning her undying affection. Stupid, immature longings that would never be revealed.

"Hey, Klein." She smiled broadly and tried to treat him like her friend and partner. It was supreme effort to act as if her pulse wasn't racing and it wasn't impossible to get a full breath into her lungs with him looking at her.

"You here to check our progress?" he asked, gesturing around at the drywall crew just getting started as they hauled in large panels of Sheetrock, and a few electricians finishing up wiring before they'd move to the next project. She'd failed to notice they weren't alone with her gaze so focused on him. They were rarely alone as there was always some crew on site, which was good.

Alone with Klein, she might say something she'd regret—or attack him.

"Yes, sir. Gotta make sure you aren't slacking."

"That hurts." Klein winked. "You know none of your men know the meaning of the word."

That wink filled her stomach with good butterflies. Her men? She'd make him her man. Oh, brother. She got so easily distracted around him. Somehow, she needed to eradicate her body of this ridiculous attraction to Klein. It had been going on for so long now that she didn't know if there was hope of extinguishing the unwanted feelings. You'd think after years of building a business together she'd become immune to his charm, kindness, and handsome face, but it hadn't happened yet.

"That's right, boss," Jared, her head drywall installer, called. The kid was barely twenty-one but he was a craftsman and worked harder than anyone on their staff. "Your dedicated crew of men work their tails off just hoping to put a smile on that gorgeous face."

"Jared," Klein warned in a low voice.

Alivia did smile. She thought Jared's teasing was funny, but she also loved the way Klein got all protective of her and annoyed when any of the guys made cracks like that. Which happened regularly. They were just teasing. Everyone knew she was the farthest thing from gorgeous.

"I'll be grinning when you finish this project on time," she said. "You know this one's going in the parade of homes, right?"

"I've heard that a time or two," Jared said. "Don't worry, our beautiful boss. We'll work night and day to exceed your expectations."

"And because you want that fat bonus," she reminded him. She paid her men higher wages than any contractor around and offered bonuses for exceptional work completed on time. It was worth it to keep highly trained and hard-working employees. Especially with how difficult it was becoming to find good men willing to do manual labor and craftsmanship. She felt like her crews and the independent sub-contractors had a great rapport with each other, and a respectful but also easy-going relationship with her and Klein.

"I'd give up my bonus for dinner with you," Jared said. His voice wasn't teasing, and the intent look in his gaze made her wary.

"Jared ..." Klein warned again.

Jared lifted his eyebrows and saluted Klein. "Yes, sir." He walked away with Tanner and she could swear he muttered, "If he's not going to take a shot, why can't I?"

Take a shot at what? Was Jared hoping for another raise?

Klein watched the two men go, then turned to Alivia. His smile was a little more forced than earlier. "Walkthrough?"

"I thought you'd never ask."

His smile became more genuine, and he gestured for her to go first. They started with the master bedroom and slowly made their way through the house, him taking notes on the instructions and ideas she'd received from her early morning Zoom meeting with the homeowners, them chatting about ways to make some of the changes work, and her trying not to notice how he smelled like sandalwood and musk.

Jared and some of the other subs teased with her as they passed, but she didn't stop to talk long. She had a new set of plans to finish up today and send to the client for final approval and a meeting with the cabinet maker at a cabin in the mountains north of here to check off on his men's work before she could cut him a check. The concrete, framing, drywall, and finish work crews were all her employees, but the electricians, plumbers, painters, cabinetmakers, countertop installers, masons, and landscape guys were self-employed sub-contractors. Most of them worked almost exclusively for her, and they had great relationships.

Klein was visibly annoyed by Jared. "Why do you let him flirt with you?" he asked in a low voice as they walked out the garage entrance and through the unfinished garage stacked with sheets of drywall, plumbing, and electrical supplies.

"He doesn't mean anything by it. He's just an innocent kid," she said, trying to convince herself as well. A lot of the guys teased with her, but Jared's behavior lately had been pushing boundaries. She risked a sidelong glance at Klein as they picked their way through the garage. "And *somebody* should flirt with me."

She'd thought the comment was teasing, but it fell flat. Klein said nothing until they reached her truck. Then he turned to her before she could open her door, his jaw working. "You're their boss," he said. "They should treat you with more respect."

Alivia shrugged. The only reason she was the head honcho and not Klein was because nine years ago she'd been willing to take a risk and the bank had happily loaned the startup capital to a Delta. With her dad signing on the note. She'd paid back the loan and was in the black now. The stress that had relieved made her smile every day. Klein had been doing remodels on his own at that point and she'd recruited him to work with her. They'd built the business together. Through the profit sharing she'd belatedly figured out and set up with him, he now owned twenty-five percent of Delta Builders. If he stayed with her, he'd eventually get to forty-nine percent. She prayed he'd stay with her. They complemented and understood each other.

Her men did tease with her, but her personality and comfort around men encouraged it. She felt like they were respectful enough, especially for a bunch of sometimes rough-around-the-edges construction workers. Klein treated her with the utmost respect, of course. She wished he'd relax and flirt a little, but that was silly, whimsical thinking, and that kind of thinking hadn't made her a multi-millionaire succeeding in a man's industry by the age of twenty-seven. She could take any tease, work her tail off, and continue to grow her business. That was what mattered, not dreaming that Klein could somehow fall for a woman who didn't know how to act feminine. She'd seen some of the beauties he'd taken out. Petite, sweet, frou-frou beauties who wore makeup, dresses, and heels. Basically her complete opposite.

"I'd rather have a good rapport with them than demand respect. They're construction workers, not exactly manners experts."

He looked her over. "Alivia ..." She didn't like that he hadn't used her nickname. Everyone else close to her called her Livvy, but Klein always called her Ali. She loved the way he said it. "You work harder than anyone I know. You're fairer with your employees than you need to be, and you shouldn't have to demand respect. They should give it because you've earned it."

That meant a lot, and she opened her mouth to tell him so when he ground out, "The problem is you are a breathtakingly beautiful woman who is far too easy-going, generous with your employees, and fun to tease with. That's why they can't resist flirting with you."

Her eyes widened, and she had no idea how to respond to that. Klein's green eyes were focused on her as he awaited her response. Breathtakingly beautiful? Was he nuts? She finally croaked out, "You think I'm breathtakingly beautiful, generous, easy-going, and fun to tease with?"

His eyes grew wary, and he grabbed her door handle and yanked open the truck door for her. "Thanks for coming by the site," he said, looking past her shoulder at the thick pine trees. "I'm heading to the Zander job after lunch. Any specific instructions?"

"No." She cleared her throat and forced a smile. "Thanks. I appreciate all you do. Couldn't do it without you."

He met her gaze and something deep in his green eyes made her stomach flip-flop happily. Could it be possible he was ... interested in her?

"Anything for you, Ali," he said so softly she barely heard him.

Her smile became so big her cheeks hurt. Did he mean that? Heat, hope, and unimagined possibilities filled her. She was terrified she was reading too much into this because of how gone she was over him.

"Are you coming to the barbecue and dance tomorrow night?" she rushed to ask, wishing she dared ask if he would dance with her. That would push boundaries, though. Right? What about him saying she was breathtakingly beautiful, and he'd do anything for her? Those weren't comments he'd ever made before. Did she dare believe them? Had something changed? Did she dare hope? Was he ready to push boundaries? Maybe his sister Shelly getting engaged to Alivia's cousin Thor a couple weeks ago had made him realize he wanted to find the right woman for him. Could she be that woman? Oh my, she needed to stop her silly girl thoughts. Klein could have any woman he wanted. She wasn't his type, and she would get her hopes up just to have them dashed.

"Do you want me to come?" he asked.

"Yes," she admitted before she could stop herself.

Her Papa hosted barbecues often in the summer at the family's beautiful picnic spot at the edge of the lake. Klein rarely came as he and his sister Shelly took care of their grandmother who had dementia. They had nurses that split the day shift Monday through Saturday, but they worked together to be there for her at night and on Sundays. She'd overheard the afternoon nurse Kelsey at the grocery store claiming Klein was "adorable with her little boy, Mo, and showing lots of interest in both of them." It had made Alivia jealous, and also made complete sense. Why wouldn't Klein be interested in a five-four, absolutely exquisite single mom who cared sweetly and attentively for his grandmother? It made a lot more sense than him being interested in an Amazon woman who fit in with roughneck contractors. Who Klein wanted to date was none of her business, but she didn't know how to stop her unreasonable feelings for her manager and business partner.

"I'll see if Granny is up to coming," he said.

"Sounds good. Papa's smoking brisket, trout, and chicken. Don't tell him I said so, but his trout should be world famous." She grinned. She loved teasing Papa that his food wasn't famous, but it was absolutely delicious.

"Can't wait," he said.

She could hardly wait to see him outside of work. Her younger sisters Jessie and Madison would both be in town. They both occasionally suggested they could help her with her makeup and hair if she ever wanted. She'd never wanted. But if Klein honestly thought she was breathtakingly beautiful in a work shirt and her favorite cargo pants that concealed her knives ... what would he think if she dolled up? He saw her in a dress on Sundays, but she always wore a comfortable cotton dress that didn't show off her shape and put her hair in a bun instead of a ponytail.

What if? She couldn't believe she was allowing these thoughts, but once they poked their way in, it was impossible not to wonder. Could she be beautiful to him? It had always been easier not to fuss with makeup and wear a work shirt and pants, but sometimes she wondered how it would feel to get dolled up, and especially have Klein look at her in awe and wonder. She'd rarely been asked to Homecoming or Prom like her sisters. All her friends had been boys, and she'd helped them ask other girls to the dances, occasionally getting the charity invite from one of them. She hadn't cared. She and Papa had gone on hunting trips those weekends instead. She didn't need to be Cinderella, but the thought of looking beautiful for Klein ...

She shook her head, steeled her jaw, and tried to focus on reality.

She stepped toward her truck, but Klein didn't move back. Their bodies brushed, and awareness sizzled through her. What would it feel like to be held against that muscular chest of his, resting her head in the crook of his neck, kissing his stubbled jawline and making her way up to his lips? She had no idea what kissing felt like, but she could imagine a kiss with Klein would be sensational.

"Ali?" Klein stared down at her, so close, so delicious-smelling, so handsome.

Her breath shortened, and she stared into his green eyes. Her usually-rational, too-work-focused brain had vacated the spot between her ears. Their gazes caught and held, and she found herself easing so close that the lean lines of his body pressed against hers. Heat filled her. She'd never known a feeling like this. It was delicious and intriguing, and she wanted this man closer.

A door slammed and loud voices approached from the garage. Alivia was jolted back to the present. She scrambled into her driver's seat, face flaming hot, and tugged at the door handle.

Klein backed away and lifted a hand. "See you tomorrow." They both pulled on the door, and it slammed shut with a resounding and final bang of metal.

Alivia couldn't even look at him. She prayed for strength and to get her head on straight. What had just happened to her? She'd contained her attraction and admiration for Klein for years. A little compliment from him and a brush of his body, and she acted like an irrational teenage girl. Was she that desperate for someone to think she was beautiful? No, she'd heard she was beautiful from other men and known they were just blowing smoke. Klein saying she was beautiful and looking at her with those green eyes stole the oxygen from her lungs and the practical brain from her head.

She pushed the button to start her truck and jammed it into reverse, looking into the backup camera as she eased away. She made the mistake of glancing out the front window before she dropped the truck into drive. Klein was watching her, and his expression was full of longing. Her heart raced.

Was she alone in her silly crush, or was there a possibility her work partner shared her feelings? She didn't know if she dared find out. It wasn't only dealing with the messy work possibility if they got involved. If he didn't feel the same, she could make things extremely awkward and possibly lose her friend and her hardest-working and most loyal asset. If he didn't share her feelings, her heart would be irreparably broken.

Was all of that worth putting her heart out on the line? Probably not. It was all too scary and risky. She'd been trained to fight by Papa, who was a military specialist and ex-Admiral. She wasn't afraid to fight, work hard, or succeed in a man's world, but she was terrified to expose her feelings for Klein.

CHAPTER TWO

Klein felt his anticipation mount as he pulled his truck into the gravel parking area in the Deltas' valley east of Summit Valley Saturday night. It was a beautiful spot with thick green mountains shadowing a pretty mountain lake and each of the huge houses owned by one of the Deltas he and Alivia had either built or remodeled.

He looked around the group of people by the pavilion but couldn't spot the tall, beautiful blonde who'd captured his heart. Her long hair would be in a ponytail and she'd be in her standard jeans or cargo work pants, but instead of her Delta Builders T-shirt, she'd be in an oversized men's T-shirt. No matter what she wore, he'd think she was breathtaking. Those bright blue eyes of hers with naturally long eyelashes, her full pink lips and smooth skin. He could never get enough of looking at or talking to Alivia.

He'd worked closely with Alivia Delta for almost ten years now. Through profit sharing, he'd worked his way into being her partner. He'd never be worthy of her, but he knew she trusted him and turned to him for work matters. He wanted to be the man she trusted her heart to and could someday love. You'd think through all their shared experiences he'd grow some nerve and ask her out. Nope. She was the most beautiful, kind, and fun woman in the world and he was the most dim-witted man with a tongue that didn't function at the moments he desperately needed to flirt and bestow witty compliments.

He smiled over at Granny. Thor, Alivia's cousin, had come to pick Shelly up earlier. It was a slice of heaven to see Shelly truly happy and engaged to one of the best men Klein knew and a close friend of his. She and Thor would be very happy. He didn't know when they would get married, and he was concerned about how he'd take care of Granny without Shelly around, but it would all work out.

He'd probably have to hire another nurse to take the early morning shift that Shelly usually covered. Good thing he was now getting twenty-five percent of the net income of Delta Builders, and his salary and bonuses were very generous. Granny's medications, doctor bills, and all the in-home nursing care were putting a serious dent in his savings account and his hopes of buying into full partnership with Alivia quicker. He should consider starting his own business, but he couldn't let Alivia go. He hated the thought of not working with her. They complemented each other. Her vision, brains, and work ethic and his execution and attention to detail couldn't be replicated.

He couldn't give up on Alivia. Even if it was rough spending his days working with the woman he loved but could never have and listening to her laugh easily as the crew members flirted with her.

Somebody should flirt with me.

He could picture her blue eyes twinkling as she'd said that yesterday. Dang, he wished it could be him who flirted with her. He was afraid if he let down his walls around her, his desperate longings and undying dedication to her would gush out. She'd think he was insane for how deeply he loved her.

He *was* insane to not make his move. He needed her in every part of his life and had no idea how to make it happen.

He jumped out of his truck and walked around to help Granny down, easily lifting her to the gravel. She weighed less every day. It was another worry.

"You look so pretty, Granny," he said.

"Oh, my handsome boy." She slid her hand through the elbow he offered, and thankfully she didn't look anxious. She preferred being at home and rarely left the house besides church. He hoped he wasn't being selfish bringing her here tonight, but when Alivia had specifically asked if he'd be here, it was hard to resist coming.

He'd asked Granny last night, and she'd said she would love to go. So here they were. Granny in her Sunday dress, the white one with flowers on it, and a floppy hat that made her look like a Southern woman. Shelly had brought their side dishes with her so he could just focus on getting Granny to the party. Klein's parmesan breadsticks and a chicken and pecan summer salad would both be gone before he went through the line. Granny had taught Klein to be a fabulous cook. If only he could cook for Alivia and make her fall for his culinary skills.

They strolled down the slope to the large pavilion where most of the town was gathered. They must've missed the prayer, as the ladies were already getting plates and walking to Papa Delta, who was proudly dishing up his smoked meat delicacies. Klein's mouth watered.

Thor saw them and waved Klein over.

"Granny Vance," Papa Delta boomed. "You come to the front of the line, you sweet angel."

Granny stopped walking and looked up at Klein. "What's the name of that man calling to me?"

Klein's stomach dropped. Granny's dementia was progressing, and she often forgot what she'd been about to do and sometimes had trouble remembering a recipe that she would've known by heart, but to not remember Papa Delta?

"It's Papa Delta," he said carefully. "Davidson Delta. He's your friend, and this valley is owned by him and his family. His grandson Thor is marrying Shelly."

She stared at him and then comprehension came, and she nodded. "Of course. Sorry, my handsome boy. I get confused sometimes."

"It's okay, Granny. No worries." But it scared him. When would she forget him and Shelly? She was the only one the two of them had left, with their mom abandoning all of them as young teenagers, their grandpa dying long before that, and then their dad dying just last year.

They walked over to the line and met Shelly. Friends called greetings. Shelly handed over a plate and asked, "What's wrong?"

"Nothing." Klein shook his head and put on a smile. He'd tell her later... or not. Shelly did too much and wore herself out. She didn't need any more stress. Admittedly, she'd been happier the past two weeks than he'd seen her in the past year. He didn't need to take the genuine smile off her face. He liked seeing it a lot more than the fake one they were both experts at.

Many people said he and Shelly looked like twins with their dark hair, tanned skin, and green eyes. He took that as a compliment. His sister was gorgeous. And he was tough enough he could handle being called a "pretty boy." He smiled to himself, thinking of the times he'd knocked an opposing team member to their back after they taunted him with that on the football field.

"Have you seen Alivia yet?" Shelly asked, walking with them in the line.

He looked around again. "No. I haven't seen her." Disappointing. Why would she ask him to come and then not be here?

Shelly's eyes got a beguiling light in them. She tilted her head and looked over his shoulder. "Hi, Livvy."

"Hi, Shell." The lilting voice he'd know anywhere came from behind him.

Klein whirled around and about knocked his sweet grandmother down. He steadied Granny and stared slack-jawed at the woman of his dreams. "Ali," he managed, his voice all husky and breathless and far too telling.

She smiled, tilting her head to the side and causing her long, shiny blonde curls to cascade over her bare, tanned arm.

The woman standing in front of him was definitely Alivia, though he wondered briefly if she was an alternate-universe version of herself.

Alivia's long hair was in smooth curls that framed her perfect face and trailed down her arms and back. She had some of that eye stuff on that made her lashes longer and her blue eyes look beguilingly bright and large. He could get lost for hours in those eyes. She had shiny stuff on her lips, too. He loved her naturally pink lips, but with that shiny, sparkly stuff, they attracted him like a moth to a flame. He'd give anything to feel the pressure of those lips on his. Did that shiny stuff taste good? He didn't care. A kiss from Alivia would taste better than brisket, steak, ribs, anything he'd previously thought he loved.

The clincher was her dress. He knew Alivia was fit as he'd seen her toned arms working as hard as any man could, but she always wore her work shirts and carpenter pants. He had absolutely no idea she had a shape like this. The dress was fitted—very, very fitted. The material outlined and clung to her curves in all the right ways. It had a V-neck, no sleeves, and stopped above her knees. The smooth skin of her arms, shoulders, neck, and legs was revealed. He wanted to take her in his arms and feel each curve pressed tightly to him, trail his lips down that smooth, elegant neck.

He would be seeing this image of Alivia in his daydreams and night visions. If he'd been smitten with her before, now he was enchanted as if she were a sorceress and had complete power over his simpleton of a mind.

"What do you think?" she asked, the teasing in her voice that he loved to hear directed at him.

"Think?" he managed. There was no thinking happening in his brain. All he could do was gawk and wish with everything in him that this woman wasn't his boss, his partner, his longtime friend, completely unaffected by him, and off limits.

"Wow," Granny said. "Isn't she a wolfy lady?"

"Do you mean foxy lady?" Shelly asked. Granny often mixed up her words.

"Sexy woman," Granny said, laughing at herself.

Klein completely agreed. Alivia pulled her lower lip between her teeth in the most intriguing move known to womankind, and he shoved a hand through his hair. What on earth could he say that wouldn't give him away? She'd know exactly how gone he was over her if he opened his fat mouth.

"Klein." Shelly elbowed him in the gut.

He looked at his little sister and could easily read the demand in her green eyes. He needed to give her friend and his boss a compliment. If he didn't figure it out and quick, Shelly was going to short-sheet his bed tonight or put dirt in his brownies.

"I've got Granny," Shelly said, smiling at Alivia. "You look absolutely gorgeous, Livvy."

"Thanks, Shell."

Shelly turned away with Granny, and Thor hurried up to help

them get a plate of food for Granny. He whistled when he saw Alivia. "Sheesh, cuz, you clean up nice."

"Thanks, Thor."

Several other people walked by and complimented Alivia. She shyly thanked each of them, sneaking looks at Klein every time. He stood there next to the line that was snaking by them as people gave the woman of his dreams compliments, and he felt like he'd gone mute. All he could do was stare at her perfection and wish he could hold her close.

She backed away from the line, and he followed her. He wanted to beg her to forget dinner, walk into the forest with him, and he'd show her exactly how gorgeous she was. But he shook his head. He couldn't do that. He'd jeopardize their friendship and maybe get himself fired and what if ... His gut churned. What if she'd dolled up for Jared or one of the other guys they worked with or one of Thor's cowboy buddies or the sheriff or any number of men who would give their tools up for a date with her?

He edged close to her. People still in line and those eating were probably gawking at the two of them. No, they were gawking at Alivia. It wasn't just that she never dressed up, but with her hair down, a little makeup on, and that dress highlighting every curve, she'd taken her natural beauty to otherworldly. She looked angelic, ethereal, perfect, irresistible ... Why could he think these things but couldn't spit them out and then tell her he loved her and had for years? He was going to come across as a stalker or a pathetic loser if he admitted how long he'd loved her and how desperately. How could he ease into this and not bungle it up?

"What do you think?" she asked again, blinking up at him and studying him as if his answer meant everything to her.

"I, um ..." He brushed at his hair again, shifting from foot to foot. "I've never seen you all fancied up," he managed. He wanted to smack himself. He was blowing this. His mind was a mass of confusion about the best way to proceed, but he could easily sense he was doing the exact opposite of that.

He had to be able to give her a compliment without telling her he was desperately in love with her. Without begging her to marry him. He'd never tell her his true feelings. Maybe when he was her equal partner or if he could somehow find out she cared for him a fraction of how he cared for her. Maybe then he'd be confident enough to take the leap and somehow survive if she rejected him.

She waited for him to spit something out. Alivia was a tough, fun lady who could take a tease and liked to tease back. He'd never seen her come close to being unsure of herself or getting emotional. He could swear at the moment that her blue eyes were getting brighter and her lip was trembling. Was it something he'd said or done? Or failed to say or do?

Heaven, please help me, he begged.

Laughing uneasily, she shrugged her trim shoulders and said, "It's a pretty silly joke, right? Maddie and Jessie thought it would be fun to dress me up. I'm like their Barbie doll or something."

She was much prettier than any Barbie doll.

"I thought it'd be funny since everyone always sees me in work clothes." She grinned as if it was all a joke, but her voice was shaky. "Really funny, right?"

"Ali ..." He moved in closer, inhaling her light, clean scent. He didn't think she wore perfume, but he loved how she smelled like clothes fresh from the dryer.

She blinked up at him and moistened her lips. "Yes?" she said, softly and sweeter than he'd ever heard her say anything.

"You may have meant it as a joke," he said roughly, his voice hoarse and scratchy, praying he could get the words right and tell her how gorgeous she was without revealing the depth of his longing, messing up their friendship, or getting fired, "but for me, you look—"

"Livvy, my girl," Papa Delta's voice boomed from far too close. "You and Klein come eat. Everybody else has dished up and I'm ready to stop serving and eat myself."

Klein's shoulders lowered. He stared at Alivia, but she'd already turned away and walked over to hug her grandfather. Klein pivoted, not wanting to let her out of his sight for an instant. He'd never seen her legs uncovered before. They were strong and shapely. Whew. Just watching her walk made his hands shake. Alivia was confident, tough, and in charge of the world. His world, at least.

"Thanks, Papa." She grabbed a plate and let him dish her up trout, chicken, and ribs. "This looks delectable."

"Not as delectable as you look, sweetie. You all dolled up for someone special tonight or just celebrating my world-famous trout?"

"Not even Colorado famous," she teased her grandfather. Her gaze slid to Klein and held. The world and everybody in it fell away. He focused on her beautiful blue eyes, praying she'd see how beautiful she was simply by the look in his own eyes. She turned away and smiled up at her grandfather. "No one special. I just finally gave in and let Maddie and Jessie have some fun dressing me up."

Was that just an excuse or had she really only thought it would be fun to dress up and shock everybody? She loved to tease and pull pranks at construction sites. Not long ago, she'd taken all the tires off their finish work guy's truck and left it suspended on four jacks.

Was this just another joke? He hoped it wasn't. He wanted to see her like this every day of his life. But he thought she looked "stop-dead gorgeous" in Granny's words in work pants and a T-shirt with her hair in a ponytail.

"Well, you look stunning, my beauty."

"Thanks, Papa." She kissed his cheek, then sashayed past Klein. He watched her go with his heart thudding hard against his chest and all kinds of compliments trying to get loose from his tongue. He'd failed. He'd had her one-on-one, had the chance to gush compliments about her and then beg her to love him, but he'd missed it. Missed it worse than slamming a hammer against his thumb instead of into the nail. His thumb would heal. His heart wouldn't.

"What'll it be, Klein?" Papa asked.

"Oh." He numbly took a plate and eased over to the three huge smokers. "I'll try some of each."

Papa Delta put the meat on his plate and eyed him perceptively. "Granny doing okay?"

"Not really, sir," he managed.

"You doing okay?" Papa's compassionate voice tugged at him. All the Delta family treated him like family, but it was Papa he thought of as a role model. His own father had been no kind of role model after he turned to alcohol to kill the pain of his wife ditching him, and Gramps had been gone too long for Klein to remember much that he'd taught him.

Klein nodded quickly. "Yeah. Just busy. Your granddaughter's a hard worker, and I try to keep up." He couldn't resist looking over his shoulder. Alivia was filling up her plate with side dishes and none other than that idiot Jared was at her elbow. Klein cursed under his breath.

"You've got it bad, eh Klein?" Papa stepped close to his side, staring at Alivia as well.

Klein tried to school his features and clear his throat. He had no idea how to respond, but he wasn't about to admit he loved this man's granddaughter when he couldn't even tell Alivia she was beautiful. If Alivia somehow heard through the grapevine that Klein loved her, it would mess up things at work, but also she'd think of him as a wuss. One thing he knew for certain—any man who won that lady's heart would not be a wuss. His shoulders rounded. He'd been acting like one for years and tonight had only confirmed how wimpy he was around Alivia.

"Thanks for the meat and the party." Klein held his plate up as if in salute, meeting Papa's clear blue eyes, the same color as his gorgeous, out-of-reach granddaughter's.

"Sure thing. Glad to see you here." He leaned in closer and smirked. "And you'd better hurry, or she'll be claimed by some other smart young man." He tilted his chin toward the pavilion.

Klein should've played it cool, but he whipped around and saw Jared carrying Alivia's plate and Sheriff Reed setting a drink down for her next to where he'd been sitting. The two men helped her navigate the bench of the picnic table in her tight dress, Jared checking out her legs and making Klein's gut churn. Then they sandwiched her between them. Jace and Ammon Jardine were sitting across from Alivia, eyeing her like she was prettier than a fresh powder day at their ski resort or that new express chair lift they were always scheming how to buy. Several other men from town and from their construction crews crowded in as well. Everyone obviously drawn to her sparkling laughter and beautiful smile.

Klein's head slumped forward as if his neck muscles had lost their strength. He was too late. He made his way to the table of side dishes and put his fair share on his plate. He ended up sitting at a different table than Alivia with Shelly, Thor, Granny, Kelsey and her son Mo, and a bunch of the Delta crew. He tried to participate in the conversation, or at least look interested in what someone was saying, but all he could hear was Alivia's lilting laughter and beautiful voice as she teased and flirted with the dozen men crowding around her table.

Did she know she was torturing him? He wanted to shout to the world that he adored her, then fall to his knees in front of her and beg her to have mercy on his heart.

He clamped his jaw and steeled himself to get through this night. Somehow. Monday morning, everything would be back to normal. Did he want normal? No. He wanted Alivia Delta, and she was flirting with the sheriff, the ski resort owners, Jared, and every other smart single man in town.

CHAPTER THREE

Alivia wasn't immune to the flattery in the men's eyes at the party or the meaningless compliments. She had fun joking around with Reed, Jace, Ammon, Jared, and a few others, but her heart screamed for Klein. His gaze had said that he was stunned by how her sisters had dolled her up, and maybe that he wanted to hold her close. Unfortunately, he couldn't seem to get even the simplest of compliments past his intriguing, perfect lips. She was left wondering if she'd imagined the longing and appreciation in his gaze.

She didn't think she was imagining the admiration in the eyes of any of the men sitting around her, and she also caught some dagger looks from some women in town. She'd never done as well with female friends as male ones. She seemed to speak a different language than most women.

Her sisters were her close friends, and that was all she needed. When Maddie and Jessie asked earlier today if they could "doll" her up and she'd flippantly said, "Sure, whatever," you'd have thought they won the lottery. With as many times as they'd asked that question before a party, they had obviously been stunned by her response.

And then they had gone berserk, trimming her hair and repeating at least a dozen times how shocked they were she hadn't trimmed it in years. After the trim, they'd smothered her hair with a deep conditioning treatment. While that potion worked its magic, they'd given her a pedicure, of course stunned that she had "naked toes" without polish. Next was a manicure. They had protested but thankfully listened and buffed her nails and kept them natural. She shuddered to imagine pink fingernails at a job site. They had then moved on to a facial, putting more goop on her face than she knew a face could take. Finally, when she was afraid they'd miss the party completely, they'd rinsed out and blow-dried her hair, picked out the perfect dress from Jessie's closet, curled her hair, and put on makeup.

When she'd stood in front of Jessie's full-length mirror at her parents' house, she'd had to admit they'd done a bang-up job. For the first time in her life, she felt beautiful. She'd been excited to see everyone's reactions. If the shock was too much, she'd figured she could claim it had been a joke.

She hadn't gotten nervous until she saw Klein and then her nerves had been warranted, as it had gone all wrong. Dang it! Why couldn't he have showered her with compliments like everyone else who got within ten feet of her? She'd had this lovely though unrealistic vision of Klein telling her she was beautiful and then asking her on a date. She'd known it would never happen, but it was fun to dream.

Papa had interrupted right when she thought Klein was going to admit she looked pretty. From there, was love and devotion too much to dream of? She had no idea how relationships worked, and she would not be the one to make the first move and mess it all up with the perfect Klein Vance.

The evening progressed, and she talked and laughed and flirted and kept one eye on Klein. Every time she looked his way, she caught him studying her. It bolstered her confidence. But how could she get him to come to her? She realized too late that Klein was sitting by the sweetheart nurse Kelsey. Dang. Why would he even glance at Alivia with a woman like Kelsey around?

Somebody started music and couples began dancing on the wooden floor close to the lake. It was still light outside, so it wouldn't be super romantic, but if she could get Klein to wrap his arms around her, it would be more romance than she could probably handle.

Was she losing it completely? What if she admitted to Klein how deeply she cared for him and it got awkward? That would be idiotic. He had to say it first, and she doubted he returned her feelings.

She looked around for him and saw him gently walking his grandmother up to the vehicles. It was tender to watch him with his sweet Granny but it also meant her night as Cinderella was over. The handsome prince had done little more than give her some meaningful glances. Those glances might be all between her ears anyway. The pumpkin and the glass slipper were being smashed as she watched his strong form overshadow his thin grandmother as they walked away.

Did she dare chase after him? Offer to follow him home and help Granny Vance get ready for bed so Shelly could stay longer at the party with Thor? Alivia had helped before. Granny was an angel and everyone loved her. After Granny was settled, maybe she and Klein could sit on the couch and ... talk. Did she dare reveal her feelings for him? No, that was insane, but maybe she could lean in and kiss him, then claim it was a joke or temporary insanity if he wasn't interested.

Shelly and Thor strode up to Klein and Granny, and it appeared an argument of sorts broke out. Alivia couldn't tell what kind of discussion it was, but Klein's jaw was tight and Shelly looked to be telling him off. Shelly was feisty and a perfect match to keep Thor in line. Alivia hadn't seen her put Klein in his place recently.

Shelly must've won because Granny was looping her arms through Thor and Shelly's and heading to Thor's fancy truck, and Klein was standing alone, halfway between the pavilion and the parking lot. He pushed a hand through his curly dark hair and then he looked her way.

Everything and everyone disappeared. Klein's gaze held her captive. Those green eyes could lock on hers for hours and she wouldn't complain. His eyes were warm and full of her and giving her a better compliment than any man's tongue could form. He thought she was beautiful in this dress tonight, but Klein had told her she was breathtakingly beautiful on the job site before she let Jessie cut her split ends off and stuffed her into this too-tight dress.

What did that mean, though? When she'd asked Klein if he thought she was breathtakingly beautiful and fun yesterday morning, he'd changed the subject. And tonight he hadn't appeared capable or willing to spit out a compliment.

His jaw suddenly tightened, and a look of determination filled his face. He strode toward her, and her stomach pitched with anticipation. Her hands grew clammy, and she had to resist wiping them on her gorgeous dress.

She loved the look on Klein's face. That was the look of a brave, confident, irresistible man coming to claim his woman. Nobody had ever looked at her like that. She'd never wanted anyone to besides him. Klein looking at her in that special way made her entire body fill with happy bubbles.

An arm wrapped around her waist and whipped her around. Jared grinned at her. "Time to dance, boss." His breath reeked of alcohol. Which of her idiot drywall crew had snuck a pint in? From the smell of his breath, it was hard stuff, and it was probably a lot more than a pint. Papa Delta hated alcohol and drugs. He'd seen some promising soldiers lose their careers and sometimes their families by becoming addicted. She didn't think any of her siblings or cousins had ever touched the stuff. Except maybe Hudson. She wouldn't put anything past that hilarious and crazy cousin of hers.

"No thanks," she said, giving him a wide grin when she wanted to shove him away and see where Klein was.

"Not taking no for an answer." Jared laughed far too loudly. "You're all dolled up, gorgeous, and I'm going to show you how a real woman parties." He winked and then inclined his head. Four of his buddies surrounded her, two that worked for her, Brad and Steve, and two she'd seen around town before but they were younger than her and she didn't know their names. All five of the men lifted her off her feet, making her stomach pitch. They ran toward the dance floor, laughing like this was the best joke in the world.

Shouts of surprise and anger surrounded her. She heard Papa demand that they put her down. His voice carried, but it was far away and these idiots weren't listening to anyone. Alivia could've freed herself and done some serious damage to three of her employees, but she didn't want to draw attention to the fact that Papa had trained her to be a weapon. She was supposed to save that for intruders who tried to trespass and find the Delta secret, not alert the town to her level of training.

"Jared," she hollered over the chaos, dizziness assaulting her. "Don't make me fire your sorry butt."

They were nearing the dance floor and other couples were stopping to stare at them. Pounding footsteps sounded behind her, and she glanced back. Greer and Colt, her incredible brother and cousin, would destroy these five idiots, but it was Klein racing after her that warmed her heart.

"Give her to me," Jared demanded of his buddies.

They slid her to the ground and thrust her into Jared's arms, forming a circle around them.

"I love you, boss," Jared declared, smirking like the drunken idiot he was.

Alivia slugged him in the gut. He doubled over but straightened faster than she would've thought he could. All the alcohol in his veins must've dulled the pain.

"You have to love me," he slurred, and grabbed her hand.

She chopped at his arm and he squealed out in pain as he released her. She dodged away from him and ran into two of his friends, who shoved her back at Jared. They chanted, "Kiss, kiss, kiss!" and laughed raucously. If he tried to kiss her, she'd dismantle him.

Greer and Colt yanked the other men away from her and Jared. Klein ripped Jared back, slammed his fist into the guy's face, and then picked him up and threw him. Jared landed a few feet away in a heap, looking stunned.

"Go sober up," Klein said in a low growl that resonated through the suddenly quiet area. Alivia had no idea when the music had been shut off. "And we'll see if you still have a job on Monday." He glowered at the two other men they employed.

Brad and Steve both nodded, and one of them mumbled, "Sorry, we were just playin' around." They grasped Jared's arms, lifted him to his feet, and dragged him away as he protested and whined.

The other two men who'd been with them backed away as well. "Sorry," the one said. "Jared said his beautiful boss liked jokes. We were just kiddin' around. Sorry."

"Carrying a woman around like she's an object isn't a joke," Klein said tersely. "Get out of here."

"Sorry," the same man said. He nudged the other guy, and they both turned and hurried to the parking lot.

Alivia felt her face burn hot. She liked jokes like the one she'd pulled last week: trading out all the guy's screwdrivers for a sugar cookie decorated to look like a screwdriver. She didn't like jokes that were humiliating and disturbed the entire town. Everyone was staring at her. She'd let her sisters doll her up, and it had backfired. Instead of winning Klein's heart, she was now the awkward, embarrassed girl. She wanted to rip off the too-tight dress and hide in her house for a month.

Klein focused in on her and the embarrassment was pushed to the back burner. Klein was here for her. She had the most reassuring sensation. This man would always step in to defend her honor.

"Are you all right?" he asked.

She nodded, though she wasn't sure. His gaze didn't waver as he crossed the distance to her and tenderly touched the flesh of her abdomen. Heat seared through her at the surprisingly intimate touch.

"Your dress," he murmured.

She looked down. The waistline seam of her beautiful dress was split, showing off far too much of her abdominal muscles. She hadn't even noticed in all the commotion, but the dress was Jessie's and her sister was smaller than her. It must've split when those idiots were manhandling her. She felt humiliation flush through her anew.

"Those jerks," Maddie spit out from behind her. "You okay, Livvy?"

"I'm fine." Alivia tried to keep her chin up and put a smile on her face.

Papa stepped up close and looked her over, then shared a look with Klein. Klein nodded, and she wondered what had passed between them.

"Klein, would you walk Alivia home?" Papa asked, but he was looking at her as if asking permission for his request to Klein. Alivia was grateful for the escape as she wanted to get away from everybody staring at her, but she almost said that she knew the way home. Klein hadn't complimented her or begged to sit with her earlier. She didn't want him to be with her because he felt pity for her now.

"I would be honored," Klein said. He was also staring deeply at her, and any resistance melted away. Klein had come for her, protected her from Jared, and looked at her as if she were the only woman he'd ever want or need. Besides that, his hand had slid around to her lower back and his touch felt warm and wonderful. She was flushed, and all she wanted was to be alone with him. Somehow, she had to sort out these feelings for her business partner. Was this the moment she could finally risk it all and tell him how she respected and loved him above all others?

Alivia offered him the best smile she could with how disheveled and uncomfortable she felt with everyone watching.

He slid his arm around her waist and directed her up the grassy slope. She knew most of the town was watching them go, but she could only focus on how Klein made her feel. Her forbidden love. Or was he forbidden? She was confused by her strong feelings for him and humiliated that she'd been manhandled by her own employees. Part of her wanted to rush into her house, peel off the dress, and take a long bath, but a completely different part of her wanted to walk Klein around to her plush outdoor patio set, enjoy the beauty of her backyard and nature, and see if she dared kiss him. She was feeling so out of sorts right now that she didn't even care about the consequences.

Neither of them said anything as they walked across the long stretch of grass, then crunched up the graveled road. Her house was set off the road past Thor and Colt's houses on the north end of their small valley. Greer's house was around the lake half a mile. He valued his privacy more than any of them. Her parents', Uncle Keith and Aunt Myrna's, and Papa's houses were in the middle of the valley close to the grassy stretch, the pavilion and the lake, with the barns and corrals behind them to the east.

Klein kept his arm around her waist as they walked. It should've been awkward, but it felt comforting and exhilarating at the same time. His palm was warm and large, and it cupped her waist and hip and made her feel dainty. Every few steps, his fingertips brushed the bare skin where her dress had split and a desire and fire filled her unlike anything she'd experienced in her life.

By the time they reached the steps to her front porch, she was ready to turn into him and kiss him. It was difficult to put one foot in front of the other when all she could focus on was this man.

Klein turned to her, but instead of using his hand to guide her closer or wrapping both hands around her waist or sliding his hand up and cupping her chin or a hundred other perfect moves he could've performed, he pulled his hand back and scowled.

Her stomach turned worse than when Jared and his buddies had been running with her in the air.

Was Klein mad at her?

"Is this the first time Jared's ever acted like an idiot with you?" he demanded. "I mean, I've heard him say flirtatious stuff to you, but to manhandle you and claim he loves you and all that ... he hasn't done that before, right?"

"No." Alivia wrapped her arms around herself, suddenly chilled even in the warm late-June evening. Today had been as warm as it got in their high-elevation Colorado valley, over eighty. It was probably seventy-five still, but the trees shading her yard made it feel cooler, or maybe it was the determined yet distant look in Klein's gaze that was chilling her. "He's never touched me before."

"I think we should fire him," Klein said. "And give Brad and Steve a warning."

And just like that, she got even chillier. He was completely focused on work. They were both driven and career-oriented, but right now wasn't the time for work.

She shivered and Klein looked at her with concern but unfortunately didn't reach out to her.

"We should warn him first," she insisted, trying to be detached like Klein was doing. He'd been there for her tonight, rescued her from Jared's awkward stupidity. He'd walked her to her house all sweet with his hand on her waist and gotten her hopes up. Now they were discussing the repercussions for their employees instead of her giving him a kiss of gratitude? Ugh! "He was ripe with alcohol. I'm sure he'll be humiliated when he sobers up."

Klein sucked in a breath and looked away at her porch bursting with geraniums, petunias, and lobelia in hanging and potted baskets. She loved the smell of lobelia. He focused back on her. "Why are you defending him?"

She took a step back and ran into the white porch railing. "I'm not," she insisted. "What he did was humiliating and inappropriate, but we're both upset right now. It'll be better if we calm down and make a decision on Monday morning."

He studied her as if she had some deeper motive, but he simply said, "You're the boss."

That stung. She didn't try to push her weight around. "You're my partner," she reminded him. "And earning a higher percentage of ownership every day with how hard you work."

He regarded her as if the words weren't even a compliment. Alivia had no clue what that look meant. It was deep and probing and not one bit romantic. This night had gone nothing like she'd hoped. She hadn't sat with Klein to eat but instead had to put on a face and tease and laugh with a bunch of men she wasn't interested in while Klein sat by Kelsey. Then Jared had acted like a drunk imbecile. Now Klein had been her sort-of hero, but he obviously didn't want a kiss of gratitude. He wanted to argue with her about firing one of their best workers. She didn't want to run the drywall crew herself or find another qualified and experienced employee.

Klein's gaze suddenly softened and at the same time intensified. He looked over her face, hair, and body, then said, "I'm sorry about the way they manhandled you and your dress being ripped. You look very beautiful tonight, Ali." His voice was husky, and a tremor went through her.

"Thank you," she managed, fully appreciating the compliment he was finally able to give. She licked her lips and prayed he'd step in and kiss her hungrily.

He swallowed, and she watched his Adam's apple bob. How could even an Adam's apple be so manly and appealing? Seconds stretched slowly by as their gazes held and she thought she could read that he wanted her as much as she wanted him.

Was this finally it? Would they throw the consequences of moving past their working relationship to the wind, kiss with wild abandon, and hold each other late into the night? She could tell him all her hopes and dreams and he could return the favor. She could ask him if he liked her in this dress and if he did, she would dress up every chance she got. They could plan fun and easy dates and extravagant and involved dates. She could help him with Granny and figuring out how to give his sweet grandmother the best care possible. They could figure out things with work. They owned the company together, after all.

He suddenly broke her gaze and looked at her flowers. "Your flowers look amazing," he said.

Alivia blinked at the redirection. Was he not on the same

page? Were all her dreams just that? Destined to explode like the pipe bombs Hudson and Chandler used to make? "Um, thank you."

He swung back to look at her and cracked a half-smile. "It always amazes me how much you love your flowers when you're not much for girly stuff."

Alivia blinked at him. This conversation wasn't going anything like she'd imagined. Come on, they didn't need to pick out wedding colors, but why was he so hung up on her flowers and ... girly stuff? As if she wasn't a female?

"Do you forget that I'm even a woman?" she asked, her trembling voice probably betraying how sad that made her.

"Not in that dress," he said softly.

She blinked at him, and hot embarrassment rushed through her. Why had she let Jessie and Maddie fix her up? A dirty sow in construction worker clothes couldn't be a beautiful swan, no matter what her sisters did to her hair or what dress they squeezed her into. Wasn't the rip in Maddie's beautiful dress and the way Jared and those idiots had manhandled her proof enough that she was just playing dress-up and failing at it? It wasn't Klein's fault, but she'd let her head get all swirled in wanting to be attractive to him and had somehow imagined he'd always thought of her as a woman. Only in this dress. Not on a weekday in her Delta Builders shirt and work pants.

"Pretty silly," she managed. "Me dressing up in Jessie's dress. Kind of like my flowers, eh? It just doesn't fit the rough and tumble construction worker chick."

She forced a smile, though Klein's eyes watched her with concern and she was afraid he could see right through her. If he could see through her, did he know that all she wanted was for him to notice her? Not as a boss or partner or even a longtime friend, but as an appealing woman he couldn't resist. Why couldn't he throw any boundaries to the wind, pull her in tight, and kiss her desperately?

When he didn't respond, she continued, "You know what I should do? I should buy me a Harley, a leather vest and chaps, and take the tough tomboy to the next level." She grinned as if she loved that plan. "I'm an expert on my KTM 350. I could handle a Harley." Her KTM EXC-F was lighter than her brother or cousins' Hondas and Yamahas, but because she was lighter, she could usually keep up with their 450 motors' speed. "I like it. I'd look good on a Harley."

His eyes swept over her, and he murmured, "Yeah, you would."

Alivia got warm all over with that look and comment, but didn't that just confirm she wasn't a girly-girl? She'd look good on a Harley. She was a she-man or Amazon woman or tomboy. If Klein knew she was tasked to protect the military secret of the century, he'd know even more that she wasn't a normal woman. She wasn't the type of woman that could capture a man like Klein. She didn't see him dating often, but when he did, it was usually a petite brunette who knew how to wear a dress and rocked high heels. Like Kelsey. She'd never seen him with a tall blonde who knew how to rock a hammer and dirt bike.

Cripes. Being in love with your construction partner stunk.

"Enough of this fake dress-up night." She forced a smile. "It was a joke that went wrong. I can't wait to peel out of this skintight thing and soak in the tub."

Now his eyes filled with a fire that left her panting for air. That look said he was definitely attracted to her, even if she normally didn't act like a female. That look said he was going to finally act on his desires. Did she even want him to anymore? Okay, she did, but it wasn't smart. This entire night had been a disaster. She could blame her sisters, who were overly ambitious with lip goop and a nail file, but it was all on her. She'd gotten her hopes up. She'd thought Klein would be sweeping her off her feet and devouring her mouth with his. Fantasies like that never came true.

Silly. Stupid. Over. Done.

"Goodnight." She lifted a hand and backed up the steps, clinging to the railing for support. Her heels were only one inch because she was so tall she didn't need any help with three-inch heels, but she still felt unsteady. "Thanks for the help. Let's think on Jared and talk about it on Monday." With each word, she eased back further until she was touching her front door.

Klein nodded and gave her a smile that looked every bit as forced as her own. "Sounds great. You're sure you're all right? You don't need me to ..." He looked her over, and the blood rushed out of her head at the heat in that look. "... stay?"

Stay? What did he mean by that? Watch over her? Hold her?

No. This was Klein. He probably wanted to pop some corn and watch one of Chandler's recent lacrosse games that she had recorded on her DVR. That was their relationship. Friends. Buddies. Partners. Construction workers. Not kissers and huggers.

"I'm great. See you at church." She waved, pushed down the door handle, shoved the door open, and tripped over the doorjamb. She heard him start toward her, probably worried about her ability to walk in anything besides her Ariat steel-toed work boots. Alivia shut the door before he could get there.

Unfortunately for her, the door was made of glass.

She and Klein stood there, on opposite sides of the glass, staring at each other. His gaze said he wanted her to invite him in, to *stay,* whatever that meant. She knew how strong Klein was in his Christian faith and didn't fear for one minute he meant anything inappropriate by it. Knowing the steadfast, loyal man in front of her, he only meant that he would be there for her, as he always was. But usually he was there for her as a manager and partner and friend. Not as the man who made her heart race.

She leaned into the door and feasted on his green eyes. For a long, beautiful moment she wondered if she dared step back, swing open the door, and ask him to make all her girlish fantasies come true.

Girlish. She wasn't a girl. Well, she was, but she'd never behaved like one. Her brothers would probably be shocked to know she had girlish dreams and tendencies and in her weak moments allowed herself to dream about the "suave, sexy stud" standing on the other side of her glass door.

Dang it, Jessie. Alivia needed to stop thinking of the nickname Jessie had made up for Klein and she needed to stop letting Jessie talk her into dumb things like putting on this beautiful dress and all the other hoopla.

Her fingers went to the rip in the dress. Klein's gaze dropped to the spot as well.

Embarrassment filled her. She'd made a fool of herself dressing up tonight and having Jared and his buddies treat her like a plaything. She wasn't some empty-headed boy toy, but she also was the furthest thing from a gentle, sweet girl. She was a construction worker and a businesswoman. She was analytical and tough, but she loved to joke too. Klein deserved the biggest sweetheart around. He deserved someone like Kelsey. She could instantly see Klein and Kelsey together with Kelsey's adorable little boy in the picture. It stung and helped her stay grounded.

Before Klein's eyes lifted to hers again, she spun and hurried up the grand staircase to her master suite. She couldn't get out of this dress soon enough. She'd never make the mistake of putting on makeup and thinking she could behave like a "girl" again. It only made her want Klein more and made her realize all over again that it would never work out between them.

Their business relationship was going fabulous. What kind of entrepreneur who'd put everything into her company her entire adult life would risk her success for a chance at love and romance with the perfect man? Not this one. No way. She was way too smart to make a dumb move like that.

But as she stopped in front of a mirror in her hall and fingered the big hole where Klein's fingers had brushed the skin of her abdomen and made her tingly and warm, she felt like she'd missed the opportunity of a lifetime.

CHAPTER FOUR

Klein had the hardest time walking away from Alivia's doorstep Saturday night. He watched her until she disappeared up her grand staircase, then he sank into her porch swing and just sat for a while. It was crazy how well the two of them communicated about work, sports, family, religion, or any number of subjects, but when it came to heart matters, he became a fumbling idiot and messed it all up. He'd had chances to tell her how he felt, possibly to even pull her close and kiss her. He'd missed each opening.

Well, he thought he'd had opportunities. Maybe he was deluding himself because he loved her so much and foolishly imagined the stars in his eyes were reflected in hers. One thing was for certain; he'd never forget how beautiful she looked tonight or the way it had felt to have his arm around her.

Had he really let his fingers graze her bare stomach? That had been dumb of him. He'd either messed up his chances by that immature move or embarrassed her. Probably both.

Maybe that brush of the fingers had nothing to do with it and he simply had no clue how to secure a woman's heart or make her feel loved. He was probably just like his dad.

Klein had been the only one to talk to his mom that awful night, before she'd ditched them all. He had been fifteen and getting home late from messing around with his buddies. He'd rushed into the house as his mom had snuck out to meet the bull-riding champion and steal away with him.

She'd looked Klein over and told him he would probably be more handsome than his father, but probably just as clueless about how to keep a beautiful woman happy. His mom had been almost as beautiful as Shelly now was. He'd adored her and had no idea what to say or do when she'd given him a final hug, kissed his cheek, and then walked away without looking back.

Klein had been stunned that night. His mom had always been fun and reasonably affectionate. He would never understand what had prompted her bitter words and her leaving them all behind. He knew the issues were between her and his dad, but it still ripped him apart to get ditched by his mom.

He'd never told anyone about the exchange that night. What would it have accomplished besides more hurt and self-blame? There had been enough of that to go around.

The entire family had gone through denial, anger, and shattered hopes. He didn't know that any of them had ever come to peace with it. His dad obviously hadn't. Instead of chasing after his wife, he'd turned to alcohol. A year ago, he'd walked off a cliff stone drunk. Granny had seemed to deal with everything the best, praying and being an example of a true Christian and being there for and loving Klein and Shelly. He thought Shelly had done pretty well over the years without a mom, until Dad died, Granny got dementia, and then her horse got injured. But now Shelly was in a great place thanks to Thor and his undying devotion. He had helped her see her self-worth and that she didn't have to fight through life on her own.

Klein buried his head in his hands. He was the one who was a mess. Most people assumed teenage boys didn't want to be around their parents, but he'd sure needed his. An awkward, growing boy without a mom to hug him and think he was the greatest thing in the world, or a dad to keep him in line and teach him to be a man. His dad hadn't died until last year, but the alcohol had taken him away from Klein long before then.

Had his mom's bitter words been prophetic? Maybe Klein would never be enough for Alivia, no matter how much he wanted to love and be there for her.

He finally got to his feet, walked down the gravel road to his truck, avoiding anybody trying to catch his gaze from the party, and drove home. Shelly and Thor had Granny settled and were snuggled on the couch. He said goodnight and hurried down the hall to his room before Shelly could launch into questions. Brushing his teeth, he said a hurried prayer, undressed, stretched out on his king-sized bed, and failed to sleep.

The next morning, he was up early. It was a Sunday, so he wouldn't lift weights or work. Sundays should've been a relief and rest for him, but often he felt useless, caged, and bored. He hated to admit that going to work early and working extremely hard helped him deal with the hours of being stuck at home with his sweet Granny. He hated what the dementia had taken from them almost as much as a certain rodeo bull rider and the alcohol.

He wasn't sure what to do with himself this morning. He walked around their property for a while, pulling any stray weed and picking up broken branches from the wind. He took care of Shelly's horses and watered the outside flowers, then took a shower and got dressed for church. He wandered out into the main area and began making waffles and cheesy eggs for Granny and Shelly.

Shelly came out of her room first, looking gorgeous in an off-white lacy dress and her best turquoise boots. The color set off her dark beauty, and her green eyes sparkled mischievously. "So ... I've been dying to know," she drawled out the words, "how was the Mac-daddying?"

He needed Granny to wake up and provide a buffer from this line of questioning. "We'd better get Granny ready so she can eat. We don't want to be late for church."

"No kissing?" Shelly's face fell. "I was so certain you two were going to finally figure out the sparks shooting between you last night. She looked off the charts in that dress, right?"

"The most beautiful woman I've ever seen," he admitted, then turned back to stirring the orange juice.

"I knew it," Shelly crowed. She hurried to his side, glancing at the kitchen clock. "I can get Granny ready quick. She had a bath and washed her hair last night before the party. Spill the details."

"It all imploded, sis." He'd almost forgotten that Shelly and Thor left the party before the mess. He sank onto a barstool and told her about the idiot Jared and his buddies manhandling Alivia. Then Klein admitted to all the ways he had messed things up before and after that.

He finished, and Shelly just looked at him. "I'm sorry about Jared acting like a lame brain, but how the stink did you mess up that many chances to tell her how smitten you are, pull her in close, and kiss her? Have all the hours with a hammer pounded the brain cells right out of that handsome head? She probably thinks you don't even like her."

"How am I supposed to know what a woman thinks?" he spit out before he thought better of it.

Shelly's eyes flashed dangerously. "What is that supposed to mean?"

Klein blew out a breath and stood, taking the loaded plate of waffles and shoving it in the microwave to warm it up. The eggs were in a covered pan on the stove and should still be warm.

Shelly strode around him and poked a finger in his face. She was such a feisty beauty, and he adored her, but sometimes he needed to keep her at arm's length. "I know I'm not the only one mom messed up with her selfishness." Her shoulders lowered and instantly the fight went out of her. He could thank Thor for bringing the softness back to his sister. The real Thor, not the action hero.

She wrapped her arms around him. Klein returned the hug. She was the only one who could truly understand.

"I'm sorry," she murmured against his chest. "I'm sorry she hurt you."

There was no need to clarify who "she" was. How could a mom leave her children and never look back? Especially a mom who'd been loving and involved? Their mom obviously had her own demons she was fighting and their dad hadn't fulfilled whatever she needed. But he still didn't think it was any excuse for leaving rather than fighting for her marriage and family. He often found himself judging and picking apart his mom and her selfishness, but it accomplished nothing, so he tried to pray and give it over to God.

Granny's door opened, and they pulled apart. Granny wouldn't mind them hugging, but even with the dementia, she could still be perceptive and might notice the somber mood. Shelly hurried to greet their grandmother, and Klein started getting a waffle ready for her.

Breakfast and getting Granny ready went fine, and they made it to church on time. Sometimes Klein dreamed of a change in their schedule, of not working long hours and then caring for Granny every moment he was off work, but that wasn't reality. At least not his reality. He enjoyed his work, especially any chance he had to be around Alivia, and Granny meant the world to him. She'd raised him and Shelly after their parents had both checked out of their lives. He'd never turn his back on her or bemoan caring for her. He enjoyed their time together, but he wouldn't have minded going on a dirt bike ride, a hike, or shooting guns with Alivia after work. He loved that Alivia was interested in the same things he was. If only he could get her interested in kissing him and declaring she loved him. Like those two things would ever happen with the tough, irresistible woman who held his heart in her calloused hands.

He walked into church with Granny holding onto his arm. Thor had been waiting for Shelly in the parking lot and they were happily flirting before they came inside and calmed down.

His eyes zeroed in on the two benches the Delta family usually filled. Alivia was right there, chatting easily with her older brother Colt and his girlfriend Bailey. Colt was the town doc and a friend of Klein's. Bailey was from Chicago but had come here to write stories about small town life. She'd fallen for Colt and was working at Blake's Grill and writing her stories.

Alivia looked stunning without even trying to. Her hair was up in a bun. He'd loved seeing her hair in those long curls last night, but the way that bun showed off her slender neck and perfect jawline was every bit as appealing, if not more. He didn't think she had any makeup on today, but she didn't need it with her big blue eyes, smooth tanned skin, and pink lips.

As if she sensed him staring, she turned slightly and focused on him. Klein had a hard time keeping a regular pattern of breathing with those gorgeous blue eyes studying him. He gave what he hoped was a confident smile and started down the aisle with Granny. He was going to sit with that beauty and somehow, someway, he would get the peanut butter off the roof of his mouth, unstick his tongue, and tell her how he felt about her.

Someone stepped in their path. Klein's gaze was temporarily dislodged from his heart's desire.

"Granny, Klein." Kelsey, the afternoon nurse who took care of Granny from three to seven every day except Sunday, stood in the aisle. Their schedule was maybe a little odd, but it worked well for them. Wendy, a bossy, older redhead, came from eleven to three and then Kelsey took the afternoon shift. If either of them needed time off, the other one stepped in and did eight hours. Granny seemed to like the change in company each day.

Kelsey was a pretty, tiny brunette, but far too young for Klein. She had a cute little boy, Mo, who came to their house most afternoons with his mom. From what Klein understood, Kelsey worked the early shift at the hospital and then cared for Granny each afternoon. Her mom kept Mo in the morning and the little man came with Kelsey to their house. Granny loved him and Shelly and Klein were great with him being there while Kelsey worked.

Klein had no idea where Mo's dad was or even who his dad was. The gossips had never figured it out, though there was some speculation about him having the Delta family's blue eyes. Chandler? Hudson? Aiden? They were all gone from the valley now, but he didn't think any of the Delta men were the type to have fun with a beautiful girl and then ditch her and their son. But who knew? Hudson hated responsibility, but the crazy extreme athlete was loyal and moral. He couldn't see any of the Deltas not claiming their rights as a father.

"Come sit with us," Kelsey requested.

Mo was probably six or seven. He stood and took Granny's hand. "Come on, Granny," he begged, his bright blue eyes lighting up.

Of course Granny followed. She adored the little boy and luckily always remembered who he was, even if she sometimes forgot what they did the day before, left the oven on for hours, or misplaced her cell phone outside so it got ruined by the sprinklers.

Kelsey watched her son and Granny get settled, then grinned up at Klein. She tucked her hair behind her ear and gave him a longing look that made him wish he hadn't eaten breakfast. She was interested in him. He'd feared it before as he chatted with her every day when he got home from work and she gave him a report on Granny and he teased and sometimes monkeyed around with Mo for a few minutes. The look in her eyes now confirmed it. Crap. He had a lot of women come on to him, but he'd tried dating other women and he knew it was only the tough, off-limits Alivia for him.

He glanced over at Alivia. She was staring at him with an indiscernible expression. As soon as she saw him looking her way, she turned forward on the hard bench. Dang. Would she think he was interested in Kelsey? There was nothing wrong with Kelsey. She was a sweetheart, attractive, smart, and had a fun little boy that only added to her appeal. But she wasn't the right one for Klein. How could he keep his distance from this kind nurse and at the same time show Alivia she was all he'd ever want without messing up their business relationship?

The pastor stood and he ran out of time to figure out how to escape from sitting by the pretty nurse. He nodded to Kelsey and gestured for her to slide onto the bench. Fortunately, there was plenty of room as he sat down. Unfortunately, within seconds Shelly and Thor snuck into church late and slid into their bench. Klein found himself scooting over until he was pressed into Kelsey's side as she smiled sweetly up at him. Mo found his way onto his lap, and the adorable little man was a welcome distraction. Klein got a few looks from congregation members when he made Mo laugh too loud, but it was worth it.

When Alivia glanced around, she smiled at Mo's laughter but immediately narrowed her gaze at Klein's proximity to Kelsey. He wanted to throw his hands in the air. This wasn't his doing and though he'd admittedly gotten tongue tied by Alivia's beauty last night and then frustrated with the situation with Jared, she hadn't made declaring his devotion any easier. She'd seemed far too lax with Jared, who deserved his butt kicked and fired. Then she'd claimed her looking gorgeous was all a "joke" and ultimately his dream woman had shut the door in his face and not opened it again.

He made it through church without hearing much of what Pastor Sam said. The choir sang a beautiful rendition of Amazing Grace, they had the closing prayer, and he finally felt he could stretch and move away from Kelsey. How could he explain gently that he wasn't available when it probably seemed he was? He hadn't dated much since the responsibilities with Granny made casual dating tough. Every single woman who had somehow missed the way he gazed hungrily at Alivia Delta probably thought he was prime dating material.

Thor and Shelly were holding Mo now, and Thor was teasing the boy and tipping him upside down, making him giggle loudly. Thor dramatically clapped his hand over the little guy's mouth as he lifted him upright again. "Not in church," he whispered.

Mo's little body shook with giggles.

Kelsey laughed sweetly. "He'll be higher than a kite all day," she said, but she didn't sound bothered by it. She obviously loved her little boy and the attention he was getting.

Granny looped her arm through Kelsey's. "Let's get outside," she said loudly. "Let the boy laugh as loud as he wants."

Klein loved it when Granny sounded like the Granny who raised him. He let the group walk into the aisle in front of him before saying, "I'll meet you all outside."

Kelsey blinked up at him. Her dark gaze was yearning to capture him, but he was a sucker for a particular pair of blue eyes.

He worked his way to the front of the church, against the crowd moving down the aisle to the door. He finally reached his target —Alivia, standing with her sister Maddie. Alivia's back was to him and she was wearing a shapeless cotton dress that fell straight from her shoulders to her ankles. He didn't care what she wore. He knew what curves were hiding under that dress. The church building suddenly felt stifling. He shouldn't have thoughts like those on holy ground. Maybe he shouldn't have them anytime, but this was Alivia and he couldn't stop thinking about her.

"Hi, Klein," Maddie said, leaning over Alivia's shoulder. "You're looking mighty fine in that dark-gray suit." She winked and Klein knew she wasn't flirting; she was matchmaking. He loved Maddie right now. Alivia's neck went red, and Maddie pushed at her until she turned to face Klein. "Doesn't *Klein* look mighty *fine*?"

Alivia's blue gaze trailed over him, and he was sweating again. Usually she'd tease and he could tease back, but she licked her lips and said stiffly, "Kelsey seemed to think so. Excuse me." She pushed past Klein and fled down the aisle.

Klein was frozen. He watched her go, wishing he knew how to leap over these barriers between them. Maybe his mom had been dead-on; maybe he wasn't man enough to be worthy of a woman like Alivia.

"If you're wondering about whether you should chase her," Maddie drawled from close by, "the answer is yes and please put some hustle into it."

Klein stared down at her sister. Maddie had darker skin and hair than Alivia and was half a foot shorter, but they shared the same blue eyes and naturally pink full lips. "Really?" he asked, hating to reveal his insecurities but needing some reassurance right now. Actually, he always needed reassurance. What would his and Alivia's men think if they knew their tough boss was really a needy wimp on the inside? He prayed Alivia would never see the truth. She'd run away even faster.

"Yes." Maddie shoved at him but didn't move him at all. "Sheesh, you're built like a blooming tank. If you're interested in my sister, please go make your intentions known."

He still didn't move. Terror of more rejection at Alivia's capable hands made his size thirteen leather church shoes feel like concrete blocks. "You think she likes me?"

Maddie grunted in disgust. "Klein! How can the both of you be so smart and so perfect for each other but so dumb about figuring it out?"

"I'm just a construction worker," he said. "Shelly said the hammer pounded all my good sense from my brain."

Maddie grinned, but her blue eyes flashed. "You're smart, talented, handsome, kind, and perfect for my sister. Jessie calls you the 'suave, sexy stud' and Alivia's eyes always light up when she says it. Get that tight butt of yours moving after her."

"Madison Delta." Holly, Alivia's mom, was standing right next to them. "That's no way to talk in church."

"Or ever," Joseph, Alivia and Maddie's dad, said over his wife's shoulder.

Oh, boy. How much had they overheard? Did everyone but Alivia know he was secretly in love with her?

"Sorry, Mama. Sorry, Pops." Maddie kissed her dad's cheek and Klein could tell by the sparkle in Joseph's eye that he wasn't upset. Klein doubted Maddie knew the meaning of "sorry." She was confident, fun, and almost as sassy as Shelly.

"Klein." Joseph extended his hand.

Klein shook it. "How are you, sir?"

"Wonderful. Beautiful summer day, and my Maddie is staying for another week to delight us with her unique vocabulary."

"Luckiest man in the world," Maddie teased.

"You have an incredible family," Klein said, nodding to Alivia's parents. He'd been jealous of the Delta family at times. What would it be like to have a complete family? To go on family vacations and picnics, sit together at church, help each other through hard times? Brothers and cousins who were as close as brothers? He had Shelly and Granny, and he needed to not moan about not having parents or a brother. Thor would be his brother-in-law soon. Thor was great. Would that connection to the Deltas help his cause with Alivia?

"Yes, I do." Joseph got a smirk on his face that reminded Klein of Alivia. He wrapped his arm around his wife and said, "Of course, Colton makes us proud and our girls are all incredible, smart, talented, and absolutely beautiful."

Klein felt like his tie was choking him.

"Don't you agree?" Joseph asked, his blue eyes glinting at him. "Especially regarding my oldest daughter?"

"I do, sir." What other answer could he give but the truth?

They all beamed at him. Maddie tilted her head to the side. "Klein needs to get out of here and chase after that perfect oldest daughter of yours," she insisted.

"Pardon me," Klein managed, nodding to all of them.

He spun and strode quickly up the church aisle that was all but deserted now. He made it out into the bright July sun and searched the grassy area, the parking lot, and even the nearby cemetery. There were still plenty of people milling around, but Alivia wasn't one of them and her black Dodge quad cab wasn't in the parking lot. Disappointment filled him. He wished he could chase after her, but he had responsibilities. Despite her family's encouragement, Alivia hadn't acted like she wanted him coming after her anyway.

He slowly made his way to where Granny stood with Thor, Shelly, Kelsey, and Mo. Kelsey had a hopeful look in her eyes when she saw him. He managed a smile at everyone, and it turned genuine when Mo threw himself at him. Klein easily tossed the little boy in the air, drawing giggles from the child and tender looks from Mo's beautiful mother. Ah, no. Why couldn't he get the woman he craved attention from to look at him like that?

But no, it was probably better he stayed single and focused on Granny and working to become a full partner. Work and his sweetheart of a grandmother. That was all he needed.

It sounded like a long, lonely life.

CHAPTER FIVE

Alivia was in a sour mood Sunday that she couldn't seem to kick. Mostly because she couldn't kick the image of Klein holding that adorable little Mo and Mo's gorgeous, petite, feminine sweetheart of a mother squished into Klein's side on the church bench. The three of them looked insanely good together. Why wouldn't Kelsey be interested in Klein? He was a charming gentleman, hardworking, devoted to his elderly grandmother, handsome, righteous, smart, and truly perfect. Why wouldn't Klein return the favor and be smitten by Kelsey? Kelsey was a compassionate, petite, beautiful, capable nurse who took care of Granny, knew how to wear a dress and curl her hair, and had the side bonus of being an impressive single mom with an adorable son. Argh!

She pasted on a good face for the family barbecue out at the pavilion. Papa grilled the steaks and the rest of them contributed to the spread with corn on the cob, new peas and potatoes, several squashes from the garden, a variety of salads, homemade rolls, pumpkin bars, and even Aunt Myrna's famous snickerdoodles. Everything was delicious. Alivia might tease Papa about his smoked meat not being famous, but it was scrumptious and nobody would dispute how incredible the snickerdoodles were.

She could tell that her parents and Maddie knew she was struggling. Maddie kept trying to convince her that Klein had all but admitted to being interested in Alivia to not only Maddie but to her parents too. Her sister's interpretation of the conversation with Klein after church got her hopes up, but she had no idea what to do about it. If only she were a normal girl who'd dated, kissed, and knew how to draw a man in. She joked with the guys all the time, but it wasn't flirting. She didn't think.

Thor was noticeably absent, probably off with Shelly, Klein, and Granny. Lucky sucker. Had Kelsey and Mo been invited over for their Sunday dinner at the Vances' house? Her gut churned at the thought, and then she felt a load of guilt. Klein would be an incredible husband and father, and those two deserved both. She had no hold on him and never would.

The afternoon seemed to stretch long as she played Bocce, cornhole, and volleyball with different family members. Papa was noticeably absent, and she wondered if he'd snuck into his house and taken a Sunday nap. That sounded like a brilliant idea. She was scheming how she could sneak up to her house for an afternoon nap too when Papa strode out his front door and across the grass. He stopped next to Uncle Keith and put his arm around his shoulders. They conferred for a second, then Papa turned and whistled. Talking settled and everyone turned to him. He surprised them all with, "Meeting in the conference room in fifteen minutes."

They all either nodded or responded with, "Yes, Papa."

Papa gave Alivia a fleeting smile and strode off, yanking his phone out. All she heard was, "Thor ..." before Papa was halfway up the lawn to his house again.

Papa was obviously concerned. Something was up. Alivia pushed all the worries about her relationship or lack thereof with Klein away in the face of what could only be a Delta Protection Detail emergency.

Two weeks ago, three men had come after Thor and Shelly in her barn. She wondered if those men had surfaced, or if a new threat had emerged. They'd gone years with whispers of rumors about the secret being a weapon or hidden treasure and occasionally someone searching in their mountains and the Deltas having to redirect or stop them, but the three men who'd gone after Thor and Shelly last week had felt a lot more ominous than a curious tourist, a treasure hunter who'd heard a rumor, or even Braden Moyle who'd told Bailey, Colt's girlfriend and a reporter, about a "Delta" level secret in their mountains.

Alivia helped put away the yard games, cleaned up trash, and carried a tray of leftover food to her mom's kitchen before heading for the conference room. She didn't like the idea of the threat escalating and having to deal with more people coming after the secret, but there was a thrill as well. It stunk that she wasn't feminine enough for the likes of Klein Vance, but she loved that she was tough enough to fight alongside any of her family members. Esther, Maddie, and Jessie could fight almost as good as she could, but they still wore lipstick, high heels, and had men gaping after them everywhere they went. Alivia didn't need men gaping after her. Only one man.

Gah! She couldn't think about Klein right now.

She descended the steps into Papa's basement. On the right was a bedroom, a bathroom, an interrogation room, and an observation room. The door on the left opened into a room larger than most people's living areas. It had an enormous conference table in the middle, a computer station off to one side that could reflect images onto the wall designed for that purpose, and no windows.

None of them said much as they settled into the comfortable chairs surrounding the table. There were twenty-four chairs and only eleven Deltas here today. They were missing Esther, who was a lawyer for the Air Force in Colorado Springs. She usually came on the weekend but had church responsibilities at home today. Aiden was deployed with the Navy SEALs currently, Chandler played lacrosse for the Boston Cannons, and crazy Hudson was off risking his life somewhere to gain a thousand more likes on social media. Colt and Alivia's sisters were here, plus two interesting add-ons.

Bailey sat next to Colt with his arm around her shoulders, and a few seconds later Shelly and Thor walked in hand in hand. It was understood that when one of them got engaged, they could reveal the family secret, but Bailey and Colt weren't engaged yet. Bailey had learned the secret, though, and Papa and Colt had determined she was trustworthy.

Something about Shelly being here made Alivia feel an odd hope she shouldn't feel. How cool would it be if Klein could be added to this group? He was tough enough and loyal enough to be an asset. Her hopes deflated. He was probably at his house with Kelsey and Mo. Maybe Mo was watching a cartoon while Kelsey and Klein snuggled. Even their names were cute together. She hated it. Maddie had been so certain he was interested in Alivia, but her sister had probably solicited some kind of compliment for Alivia out of him and then assumed that meant he was all over dating Alivia.

"Welcome, Shelly and Bailey, to your first Delta Protection meeting," Papa said. "We're making an exception having Bailey here, as she isn't officially engaged to Colton."

Colt chuckled and squeezed her hand. "Soon, I hope."

"Sheesh, slow down," Bailey teased. She glanced up at Papa. "Thanks, Papa. I'm truly honored you'd include me."

Bailey did look honored, but she also had a sparkle in her dark eyes, as if this was a grand adventure. Did she understand the gravity of the secret? Not yet, but she would soon. Not that any of them knew the secret besides Papa. Unless Papa had appointed a secret keeper to take over for him.

Alivia had fancied herself being made the secret keeper sometimes. She was serious and driven and could keep a secret, but she would be okay not being the keeper. It was a lot of responsibility. It still stunned her that Colt wouldn't have the responsibility, but Papa had been insistent about it not being the most obvious. She wondered if that ruled out Esther and Aiden as well as the only two with formal military training, but she had no idea.

Shelly looked a little uncertain and very apprehensive. Both those emotions seemed out of character for the tough cowgirl, but she and Thor had also been attacked by men trying to kidnap them to get to the secret. She'd already seen a bit of the darkness and terror that could come because of what the family had been tasked to protect. Alivia was grateful Papa had told them about the secret as teenagers. Protecting it felt instinctive to her now.

"I appreciate being included also," Shelly said cautiously. "And you can trust me to be loyal and never squeak a word about the secret, even to Klein." Her gaze flickered to Alivia and Alivia's stomach hopped happily. "But honestly," Shelly continued. "I don't know how to fight military men. Thor taking out those guys two weeks ago in my barn was terrifying and impressive." She smiled up at him like he was her hero. "I could never fight like that."

"We appreciate your loyalty, and you have our trust," Papa said. "I'd like you to learn how to protect yourself and your future children. Also, your input and ideas are valued by all of us. There are other ways to protect the secret besides fighting with weapons or fists. You won't be expected to physically guard the secret unless you want to."

"Thank you, Papa," she said. "I'd appreciate learning how to protect myself and others, and I guess we can see how that goes before we train me to be a lethal weapon."

A few of them chuckled at that, though they were trained to kill if necessary. Alivia hoped it would never be necessary. To her knowledge, no one but Aiden and Papa had ever had to kill someone.

Thor smiled at Shelly and squeezed her hand. Her green eyes focused on her future husband as she leaned closer to him. She looked so much like Klein it made Alivia's heart squeeze painfully. She wanted to ask if Kelsey was with Klein. She wanted to beg Shelly to find out if Klein liked her, as if they were in middle school. She shook her head. There were more important matters at hand than her lack of a love life.

"The three men who attempted to kidnap Thor and Shelly have been released on bail," Papa said without preamble. "The bail was paid by Carmel Wright, Ensign Flynn Wright's mother and a civilian."

A groan went around the table. It was upsetting the men had been released and the fact that one of their mothers had paid the money would be investigated thoroughly but didn't necessarily give them a lead.

"Their whereabouts are currently unknown, but we suspect they're still close. At least they haven't rented a car, gotten on a flight or a train, or used their credit cards anywhere outside of Denver, Aspen, and Colorado Springs."

"That's scary, but also cool that you know all of that," Bailey piped in.

Papa smiled. "I get access to what I need." He looked around the table, then pushed a button on his laptop and three men's photos were displayed on the far wall. They were all young, tough and serious-looking men, wearing the white Naval uniform with the black tie crossed loosely and tied half a foot below their neck and a white sailor's cap.

Shelly leaned closer to Thor. She obviously recognized them and didn't like the images.

"The problem is we got no information out of them when we captured them. As you all know, they are Naval cadets stationed at Great Lakes Naval Base under my friend Admiral Seamons."

Another click and an unsmiling picture of Admiral Seamons in the decorated white uniform of a higher-up and cap trimmed in gold and black filled the screen. Alivia hadn't seen him personally in about ten years. He'd aged, but she easily recognized him from the visits he and his wife, son, daughter-in-law, and granddaughter had made to Colorado years ago. Could Papa's friend be leaking info to his men? It seemed ludicrous.

"And our old friend Lieutenant Braden Moyle."

Papa clicked, and another picture came up. Alivia heard an intake of breath and looked around. Jessie was staring unabashedly at Braden. Did her sister know or maybe like the guy? Alivia remembered meeting him when he'd come to a barbecue the first of June.

She and Jessie had been up near the cave that housed the secret, making sure it was secure and no one else was around while Braden had been interrogated for going after the secret, cleared, and sent on his way. She didn't have strong feelings about his innocence or deceitfulness.

Lieutenant Moyle was also in a Naval uniform. He had short sandy-blond hair, smoky blue eyes, tanned skin, and chiseled facial features.

"Wowsers!" Maddie exclaimed. "He is a fine-looking sailor if I ever saw one." Her hand shot into the air. "I volunteer to guard Lieutenant Moyle, shadow him, interrogate him, or whatever that beautiful man might need."

"Maddie," their dad admonished.

Papa shook his head, smiling slightly. Jessie gave Maddie a sidelong glance, but said nothing. Maddie hadn't been home the weekend they had met Braden Moyle. He'd seemed like a nice guy and Alivia could admit he was handsome, but not as handsome as Klein. Not to her, at least. Maybe to Maddie.

"Unfortunately for Maddie..." Papa paused, and a few chuckles filled the room.

Maddie spread her hands and tossed her long, dark hair. "What? I can appreciate a quality male specimen when I see one."

"Maddie." It was their mom this time, her voice full of exasperation.

Alivia laughed. Her sisters had plenty of "quality male specimens" chasing after them. Maddie was just lightening the mood.

"Lieutenant Moyle is back on base," Papa continued, "and from what we can see, he is attending faithfully to his duties and the promise he made to not speak about or come after the secret." He looked at Bailey. "In your estimation, was Lieutenant Moyle a man who would be true to his word?"

"Yes, he was," she said. "He was a gentleman and would've sacrificed himself for me if I would've let him."

Colt's jaw tightened. He'd had some days a month ago where he'd thought Bailey had betrayed him with Braden, so it was probably still a touchy subject.

"I thought the same. Regardless, we're keeping an eye on him."

"Who's keeping an eye on him?" Maddie demanded.

Papa smiled. "Someone I trust. If we need a constant shadow, or protection for our *fine-looking, quality male specimen*—" Everybody laughed. "I'll consider you."

"That's all I ask. Chicago is a fabulous city for finding unique photography material." Maddie winked at Jessie. Their youngest sister was always happy and the peacemaker, but Jessie didn't seem at peace right now. Were both her sisters after this guy, or was Maddie just being a smart-aleck like usual? Jessie had actually met

Braden. Alivia wracked her brain to remember that barbecue and who Jessie had talked and flirted with. All she could remember was that Bailey and Colt had flipped the kayak that night and fell in the lake, and that Klein hadn't been there.

Papa looked around the room. "The reason for this meeting was to first inform you of the unfortunate release from prison of Ensigns Colby Newman, Flynn Wright, and Travis Reeder, but second, to ascertain if our breach is Admiral Seamons."

The room suddenly felt tense. None of them wanted to think Admiral Seamons could betray Papa and the secret. As one of the very few who actually knew the secret was more than just a rumor or a treasure hunt, it could be catastrophic if it was Seamons.

"Admiral Seamons has been your friend for how many years?" Colt asked.

Papa squinted as if thinking. "We met in 1995 and both felt an instant kinship. Twenty-seven years." His brow furrowed. "I hate the thought of it being Ross, but we have to explore every possibility."

"How do we know it is a breach?" Thor asked.

Papa shrugged. "I guess we don't. There have been rumors circulating for years, but to have Lieutenant Moyle overhear Ross talking to someone about a Delta-level secret, a conversation Ross won't admit happened by the way, and then those three jokers show up trying to attack or kidnap Thor and Shelly so they can force them to lead them to the secret... It's too coincidental, right?"

"I'm confused, Papa," Aunt Myrna spoke up.

"Yes, sweetheart?" Papa always used terms of endearment with his daughters-in-law and treated them like his own flesh and blood. His hyper-focused gaze showed exactly how much he valued their opinions. He always teased his boys that they had both "married up."

"Admiral Seamons claimed the conversation Braden Moyle overheard never happened?" she asked, and Papa nodded shortly. "First of all, you didn't pin the admiral down about it, and second, you trust this Lieutenant Moyle over your lifetime friend?"

Papa let out a heavy breath and settled into a chair. "I'm in a box, and I hate being in a box," he muttered.

Colt's gaze registered comprehension. "You promised Braden you wouldn't reveal who overheard the Admiral's conversation. When you interrogated him, you promised if he'd keep his word, his supervisors wouldn't know he'd come after the secret so there'd be no repercussions or lack of promotions on him, as long as he kept his end of the bargain."

"Exactly." Papa splayed his hands. "I can't go back on my word, and if I can't tell Ross who overheard his conversation, how can I grill him about it?"

"That makes sense," Alivia's dad said, "but how do you know that the conversation even happened? How do you know Moyle can be trusted? Wasn't he also severely ill when he supposedly overheard the conversation? It could've been someone else he overheard, or he could've been hallucinating."

Papa nodded. "Everything you said is true. I don't know if Moyle mistook who he overheard or if he made it all up and learned about the valley and 'Delta' from another source that he's secretly protecting, but ... I just don't know. I looked into that kid's eyes, and I trusted him." He glanced up at Braden's image that was still projected.

"I trusted him too," Bailey piped in.

"I'd trust him," Maddie said coyly. "And he is no kid. That there's a *man*, Papa."

Everyone laughed, and the tension dissipated. There were no answers, but the truth would come out eventually. At least they were prepared to protect the secret. It was probably inevitable that the rumors and myths would start escalating. With how good people were at intercepting data, and satellites taking detailed pictures of spots that used to be hidden, secrecy was harder and harder to come by.

Papa proceeded to talk about increased security measures and patrols. Their cameras were top of the line and would notify them of any breach, but patrols were still important in case someone had the skills or equipment to bypass the cameras.

Alivia let her mind wander. When the meeting ended, the family broke up into smaller groups. Alivia watched Thor and Shelly load into his shiny silver truck and head out. She wished she could go with them. That was silly, but she wanted to see Klein again.

She should've spent more time with Maddie since she didn't come home often, but instead Alivia went to her own house, changed into some shorts and walking shoes, and headed for the trail on the northeast side of their valley. She headed north toward the ski resort trails, needing to move and let her mind process everything Papa had said and any possible solutions to stopping the secret from being exposed or at least its safety being assured.

Then, of course, her mind swung back to Klein.

It was after six and her stomach should be rumbling, but food was the last thing on her mind. She could see the top of the main chair lift for the ski resort over the next ridge. This area was gorgeous, with lots of wildflowers and hiking and biking trails. Usually she'd see mountain bikers or hikers who'd used the ski resort's lifts to take them up the mountainside so they could either explore more terrain or have an enjoyable ride downhill, but the lifts didn't run on Sundays. She respected the owners, Jace and Ammon Jardine a lot. They were both great guys and though they were tough, adventurous type men, they took good care of their brother Bentley, who was a bit mentally and socially off.

A lone hiker crested the peak. She knew instantly who it was.

There was no mistaking those broad shoulders, long legs, the lean lines of his body, and his dark, curly hair. "Klein," she breathed out, though there was no way he could hear her.

He stopped at the top of the peak. He could just be resting, but Alivia could swear he was focused on her. They were a hundred yards apart, with a small valley between them, but it felt like his heart was calling out to her. Alivia wanted to run down this mountain trail, crash into his arms in the valley below, and see exactly how incredible being kissed thoroughly by the impressive Klein Vance felt.

He lifted a hand high in the air, waving to her or maybe flagging her down or maybe gesturing for her to meet him down in this valley and see exactly what kissing good and long felt like. Would he laugh at her if he knew she'd never kissed a boy or a man?

Alivia cringed, and her stomach curdled. Klein was too kind and too good of a friend to ever laugh at her, but he would probably feel bad for her or be embarrassed for her. She couldn't have that. She could never tell him she had "virgin lips" as her sister Maddie loved to tease her, and he'd know that if she ever kissed him. She'd most likely be inexperienced and absolutely horrific at it.

She backed away. She was being silly, which wasn't like her at all. This had been a strange weekend with Maddie and Jessie dressing her up and Jared and his buddies humiliating her, all her feelings for Klein seeming to come to a head, and then the Delta Protection cause escalating. She needed to go home, take a bath, and then eat some ice cream. She had a new carton of Phish Food waiting for such an occasion.

She lifted a hand to Klein, and she could swear he grinned at her. At least it felt like he did, but she was too far away to know. She knew him too well, knew his smile, knew how he felt about a multitude of issues. They almost always agreed, though they could argue about things as well. Could they be soul mates? Was that why she was so drawn to him and always had been?

Oh. My. Goodness. She had to stop. She pressed a hand to her heated forehead. She must have the flu or something.

Instead of rushing down the mountain in Klein's direction like she ached to do, she spun and jogged the other direction. Back toward home. Maybe some ibuprofen could take away this weird pressure in her head. Then to important business: a warm bath and ice cream.

What more could a girl want or need on a Sunday evening?

Klein's muscular arms and incredible lips.

But that was never to be for an inexperienced, tom-boyish woman like Alivia. Good thing she'd be back at work tomorrow morning and her head would be screwed on straight again. She hoped.

CHAPTER SIX

Klein woke at five to lift weights, shower, and check on Granny before he left for the day, drinking a protein shake on the way to work. He was at the Nelsons' site by six, beating the other finish work guys there. He was Alivia's general manager and partner, but his specialties were finish work and framing and he loved the times he got to join the crew and focus on working with his hands rather than supervising. He needed to work with his hands. Especially when his mind was all stirred up by one beautiful woman who seemed immune to any charms he might have. Did he have charms? A lot of other women seemed to be taken with him. Like Kelsey. Unfortunately, he wasn't drawn to Kelsey.

Alivia called about seven, outlining a few things she was concerned about, mostly that she wanted to give Jared, Brad, and Steve another chance. They talked briefly, but there was no longing, warmth, or love in her voice. Was she feeling awkward for running in the other direction rather than take advantage of their—could you call it a meeting?—on neighboring mountain ridges? That had been so strange.

Shelly and Thor had come home from some family meeting at the Deltas late yesterday afternoon and told him to go do whatever he wanted. It was their time to be with Granny. The two of them were giving each other sly looks. He was thrilled Thor and Shelly had figured things out to be together, but sometimes they were so close he was shut out of the bubble of love that surrounded them. It was fine for him to be left out. He simply wanted the same for himself.

In that vein, he'd wished he could rush to Alivia's house and pound on the door and spend the night talking with her, and if dreams came true, grow closer. He'd wimped out, driven to the ski resort, and started hiking up one of the trails instead. When he'd seen her on the other ridge, he'd raised a hand and felt the connection swell between them. He was positive she would rush down the mountainside and he'd meet her in the small valley in the middle. They'd finally be able to talk through all the things that had eluded them in the past—love, romance, a future together—after he kissed her good and long.

Instead, she'd turned and disappeared in the wrong direction.

He pushed at his hair, focusing on the nail gun in his hand and the fancy cherry wood baseboard he was installing.

The front door of the house burst open and footsteps came from the entry and into the main living room. He looked over his shoulder and his insides lit with warmth. Alivia. She was in her standard Delta Builders T-shirt and work pants with her hair pulled back in a ponytail. She looked beautiful. Their gazes met and he could swear he glimpsed tenderness and desire in her gaze.

He set down the nail gun and stood, pivoting to face her. Her mouth fell slightly open as if watching him move affected her. He liked that. A lot.

She stared unabashedly at him as he walked toward her, blue eyes filled with a yearning that boded well for his hopes.

"Everything okay?" he asked softly when he reached her.

She swallowed and pointed at his waistline. "N-New tool belt?"

He looked down, then back up at her. "No. Why?"

She licked her lips. "It looks good."

Fire rushed through him. She liked a man in a tool belt. She liked him. She had to. He stepped closer. She only had to tilt her chin slightly to hold his gaze. He loved how tall she was. He wouldn't get any kind of kink in his neck when he bent and kissed her for a very, very long time.

There were men walking through the large open area carrying baseboards, door trim, and crown moldings that had been measured and cut to fit perfectly. Klein should be installing, which was his specialty. But all he could do was stare at his beautiful boss, or partner, or whatever she wanted to be, and pray he could figure out how to make a move.

She gestured back out the front door. "Jared, Brad, and Steve would like to talk to us outside."

"Oh." His hopes deflated for probably the thousandth time with her. He nodded, gesturing for her to go first.

She turned and walked in front of him. He wished he had the right to take her hand, rest his palm on the small of her back, or wrap his arm around her. She wouldn't appreciate that as they weren't a couple, but she also might see it as demeaning her authority on the job site. Alivia teased and laughed with all her employees, but she was still the boss.

Jared, Brad, and Steve stood just off the porch. None of them would meet his gaze. Anger flashed as he saw them and remembered the way they'd treated Alivia Saturday night. Was she really going to let them off with a slap of the hand?

He and Alivia descended the stairs, and before either of them could say anything, Jared looked at Alivia and said, "I'm awfully sorry, boss. I was drunk." He gestured to his cohorts. "We all were, but that doesn't excuse it. It won't happen again."

Klein wanted to bite out that he could bet it wouldn't as he was going to fire all their butts and then thump them all at the same time so they'd know to stay away from her.

He looked at Alivia. Her face was solemn but compassionate.

"It was humiliating," she said.

Jared flinched. "I'm so sorry. I'll pay to have your dress fixed and you can dock my wages, cut my bonus, give me overtime duties without overtime pay, whatever, but please don't fire us. We all love working for you." His gaze finally flickered to Klein, then quickly away as if he could sense how close Klein was to hitting him harder than he had Saturday night. "Both of you. This is the best job I've ever had. Plus, you know Steve will break his parole if he doesn't keep a steady job."

Klein flinched. He'd forgotten Steve had spent some time in prison for robbing convenience stores as a stupid eighteen-year-old. Just old enough that he had gotten prison time rather than the juvenile detention center. The kid had an abusive dad and no mom to speak of. Nobody remembered when she'd run off. Klein should have compassion. His situation wasn't too different from Steve's. Steve had a grandmother, but she was a lot less sweet than Granny. Thank heavens for Granny, or Klein probably wouldn't have found his faith in Jesus and maybe he would've ended up in prison, or at least juvie with no direction or solid grounding in his life.

Alivia looked at Klein. She said nothing. Her eyes said it was his choice. He knew where she stood. She didn't want to fire them. Alivia was generous and forgiving, he thought to a fault, but it was also one of the many things he admired about her. She was letting him have the final say because of her respect for him and their partnership.

The silence in the yard felt thick. All three of the men looked at Klein as well. He was happy to see they were finally meeting his eye. "Alivia is much more generous than I am," he started with.

Jared flinched. Steve pushed at the dirt with the toe of his work boot.

"The cost of her dress will come out of your pay, Jared, but we won't take away the bonuses you've earned."

They all sighed in relief, but still looked uneasy. He could pay them their bonuses but still fire them.

"I can't tell you what to do after work hours," Klein continued. "But I'd recommend you all lay off the sauce as it makes you into idiots and losers."

They all nodded their agreement.

"Sorry. I was gonna say that too," Jared said as their spokesman.

"Good. You're not fired, but don't give us any reason to regret that."

"Thank you," Steve yelled. "Thank you, thank you. My grandma is gonna come and kiss you."

The tension eased and Alivia let out a small chuckle. Klein looked at her. He'd much rather have her kiss him. Much, much rather.

"Or maybe she could make you cookies," Steve offered.

"Cookies are great," Alivia said.

They all smiled, came over and shook each of their hands and then headed back to work at a job site thirty minutes away in Grand Peak Valley.

Alivia looked at Klein as they left. "Thank you. I think they'll fall into line."

"Yeah. I think Steve is a little like me. I'm glad he has a grandma like I had my granny through my formative years."

She looked him over. "I don't think you would've started robbing the Sinclairs with or without Granny."

"You never know." He winked, but gratitude for his grandmother filled him all over again. He'd do anything for her.

She chuckled. "I'd better get going. I'm meeting with the Hunsakers for a walkthrough."

"Okay. Good to see you."

She met his gaze and her blue eyes seemed warm, but that could only be gratitude he hadn't fired those three, rather than love. "You too," she said softly.

She hurried down the porch steps, to her truck, and was peeling out of the unfinished driveway before Klein could do much more than stare after her.

Had he offended her yesterday at church? Or some other time? Who knew? He'd have to ask Shelly for help, but he hated to act like a teenager who needed his sister to match-make him with the prettiest girl in school. He was a man and should be able to stand up and tell the woman he loved everything he loved about her. And if she didn't return the favor, he would also have to take it like a man. He blew out a breath. How would he handle it if that were the outcome? It was almost easier not to get his hopes squashed and not to mess up their working relationship.

Instead of racing for his truck and chasing Alivia down, he headed back to do finish work.

The day passed quickly and uneventfully. Shelly texted him about five that afternoon and told him she and Thor were going to take Granny to dinner at La Hacienda after she got off work at seven. He was welcome to come, but she knew he was behind, so if he wanted to work late, they would bring him some takeout. He opted to work late. There was so much finish work in this huge house he didn't know how they'd ever get it done by the deadline. There was also the very slim hope that Alivia would come back to the job site and he'd get to see her again.

The other guys gradually left, but his guys had set him up.

They'd gotten through all the measurements and the precision cuts with the miter saw that was temporarily setup in the four-car garage. They'd also hauled the cut pieces of wood in and left each piece close to where it needed to be installed. He couldn't do the crown moldings or trim as he'd need somebody to hold them, but he could keep putting nails in to secure baseboards. If he could get through at least the baseboards, tomorrow wouldn't be nearly as brutal.

His thoughts ran as he worked in the quiet house. He would never think to turn on music, though it didn't bother him when the guys did. Nothing much bothered him, except his mom ditching him and his inability to know if he could ever be blessed with the love of one Alivia Delta.

He heard a truck pull up, and he straightened and stretched. He strolled through the great room to head out front and see who was here. He needed a break anyway. He pushed open the solid mahogany front door and almost knocked it into Alivia. She jerked back.

"Ali, sorry." He reached out a hand to steady her. The feel of her warm, firm skin under his fingertips made his stomach lurch.

"No worries." She smiled and strode by him, leaving him aching to touch her for a lot longer than she would probably agree with. "I heard they left you all alone to do the finish work."

"It's good." He followed her back into the great room. "They made all the cuts. I thought I'd finish the baseboards tonight before I called it quits."

"I'll help you."

"Thanks."

She nodded and set to work. Klein followed her example, and the time flew by as they secured the baseboards throughout the house. Then he held moldings for the doors in place while she used the nail gun to secure them. He and the finish work team could finish the window frames and crown moldings in the morning, but they'd need ladders for a lot of them.

He and Alivia worked seamlessly together. Even a lot of experienced, skilled finish workers weren't as effective with him as she was. They didn't talk much, and that bothered him. Usually he and Alivia had a lot to chat about—work stuff, family, religion, politics, sports, whatever—and they could talk easily. Was he being awkward or was it her? He snuck a glance at her and saw her looking at him before quickly turning away. What was different tonight? Was their silence telling, and she felt different about him? Maybe it was finally his chance to step up and tell her how he felt. His stomach churned with nerves.

Darkness fell outside before Alivia set down her nail gun and said, "My arms are gonna fall off and my stomach is crying for mercy."

He smiled as he faced her.

"Can we call it quits tonight?" she asked. "I'll help you again tomorrow if you and the guys can't get finished."

He stretched his back and teased her, "We need the big boss to finish what the slackers can't get done."

She grinned and tilted her head to the outside. Something about that gesture made his heart race. She wanted to talk to him outside in the dark? She wanted him to walk her to her truck and kiss her goodnight? She wanted him to ask her to dinner? She had mentioned how hungry she was. Shelly and Thor would take great care of Granny and most likely be thrilled if he didn't come home until late. If he was with Alivia.

He hoped he wasn't imagining the interested glances Alivia was shooting his way. His pulse didn't slow down as they shut off lights and made sure all the exterior doors were locked before walking out front to where their trucks were parked side by side.

Her black Dodge and his white Ford. They loved to tease each other about which brand was better and which color was the smarter choice for a vehicle. Klein didn't really care. He just liked to have any reason to tease with Alivia.

He walked her to her truck, and she surprised him by whirling to face him and planting her back against her door so he couldn't open it.

"Thanks for the help," he said, resting his hand on the door next to her shoulder and leaning closer. He hoped he was affecting her because being in what felt like an intimate position to her had him close to a heart attack.

"Anytime." She smiled. Then she did something that made his heart about explode out of his chest. She slowly, tantalizingly, trailed the tip of her tongue along her upper lip.

Klein swayed on his feet. He hadn't eaten since lunch and he couldn't think the last time he'd stopped for water, but he didn't think a lack of sustenance was to blame for his unsteadiness.

This woman. She turned him inside out.

He planted both hands on her truck and leaned in until their bodies touched. She sucked in a breath and her mouth softened as she stared at him.

"Ali," he said, almost against her mouth. A fraction of movement and their lips would connect. He threw all worries about making a fool of himself and ruining their friendship and partnership to the wind. "Ali ..."

He prayed for bravery for him and acceptance from her. She was breathing quick, and he could feel the sweetness of her breath against his lips. He couldn't hold back much longer. He had to leap off this cliff and see if Alivia caught him or if he splatted on the ground at her feet.

"Could I—"

Footsteps pounded their direction.

"Klein!" Alivia screamed. She tried to push around him as if she would protect him from whatever was coming.

He held her back and turned to face whatever had her so concerned.

Something solid slammed into the side of his head. He crashed against Alivia and knocked her into the dirt. He tried to cushion her with his arms and prayed he hadn't hurt her. His head hurt, but luckily he hadn't passed out.

He glanced up to see three men standing over them. One had a crowbar in his hands, and the other two had pistols aimed at them. Shock rolled through him. Who were these guys and what did they want with him or Alivia? There was something familiar about them, but he couldn't place it.

"Stand up if you can," the one with the crowbar taunted him.

Oh, he could stand up, and he could thump all three of them. If they didn't have weapons, that was. Klein was tough, but he'd never had any formal defense training. All he knew was he refused to let Alivia get hurt.

His gut tightened with resolve and some fear. He might get shot in the process, but he'd face these guys like a man and somehow protect Alivia.

He whispered into Alivia's ear, "Crawl under your truck. The keys are in mine. Get out of here." He didn't have to say it. She'd call for help. He could hold them off until Sheriff Reed or his deputies got here—maybe. All that mattered was Alivia was safe. This home was in the trees almost twenty minutes from town and miles from the nearest neighbor. Nobody would hear them fighting. He had to protect Alivia on his own.

"Klein," she said in what sounded like a frustrated tone, as if he had no clue what he was talking about or maybe she thought he was trying to play hero and couldn't accomplish it. He was going to protect her. What was wrong with that?

He got to his feet in front of her, holding his hands out and wondering if he could lull them into thinking he wouldn't put up a fight. "What are you after, guys? I've got a few hundred in my wallet and my personal and business credit cards."

Even as he said it, and before Mr. Crowbar sneered more fiercely, Klein knew this wasn't about money. These men were all ultra-fit, had cropped hair and an edge that said they could and would happily thrash him. Military, police, or hired thugs. He honestly couldn't be sure which title they held.

Alivia stood next to him. Why hadn't she crawled for his truck and escaped?

"Ali." He tried to step in front of her.

"Klein." She grabbed his arm. "They're here for me."

"What?" Klein shouldn't have taken his gaze off of the men, but he had to turn and look at her. Why would three trained... some-things... be after Alivia?

He felt them edging in behind him, surrounding them. He whirled, and they stopped. But he and Alivia were pinned by the truck behind them. How would he protect her?

"Isn't that right, Ensigns Newman, Wright, and Reeder?" Her voice was even, and she didn't seem scared at all.

Mr. Crowbar smirked. "You've got a bead on us, eh Miss Delta? Doesn't matter. We underestimated your cousin. Loverboy Cowboy was a better fighter than anyone I've ever come up against, and believe me, I've been in my share of fights. We're more prepared for you, and we aren't going to prison this time."

Klein felt far behind the curve, but he realized where he'd seen these three. It was only a couple of weeks ago that the sheriff had hauled them out of Klein's barn because they'd attacked Thor and Shelly. "Loverboy Cowboy" must be Thor. He knew Thor was a good fighter, and Shelly had said it was impressive how he'd taken on all three men. Could Klein do the same? The knot in his gut said no.

"Let Klein go and I'll take you where you want to go," Alivia said in that same even, unemotional tone.

"Not happening. You'll lead us to the weapon or we'll kill Loverboy Construction Man."

Alivia leaped into the air and kicked the one on the right in the hand. His gun went flying, and he cursed and knocked into Mr. Crowbar.

Klein was amazed by the kick and took that as his signal to plow into the guy on the left who held the other gun. He went low and drove his head and shoulder into the man's chest like he'd been trained to do in football. He heard the gun discharge but didn't feel a bullet hit him.

They slammed into the ground. Klein ripped the gun from the man's hand and tossed it away. Easing back to give himself some room to move, Klein started in with sharp jabs to the guy's face.

A scuffle to his side caught his attention, and he looked to see Alivia fighting two of them at once. She looked like a machine or some hero from a Marvel movie as she punched, kicked, and dodged their hits.

"Ali," he breathed out in wonder. Her initiating jump kick had been impressive, but how had she learned to fight like that?

The man underneath him flipped Klein off him and pinned him down. Klein elbowed him and the man's head snapped back. Before Klein could execute a reversal of his own, one of the men fighting Alivia suddenly bounded Klein's direction, yanking a needle out of his pocket.

"No!" Alivia screamed, starting toward them.

The man she was fighting took advantage of her distraction, grabbed her shoulders, and slammed her back against the truck.

"No!" Klein shouted.

The man dropped to his knees next to Klein. The tip of the needle plunged into his upper arm and cool liquid flowed into his bloodstream.

Klein roared and threw both men off of him. One rolled in the dirt and the other hit the truck's tire. Klein lumbered to his feet. Was this how an injured mama bear felt? Backed into a corner, knowing he was going to bite the dust soon, and only caring that he protected his cub. It was a weird analogy, as Alivia was not his cub but the woman he loved. But he didn't care. If it was the last thing he did, he would protect Alivia.

He stormed toward the man who had slammed Alivia into the truck.

"Klein," she said in an awe-inspiring voice that filled him with more strength. He wanted to pound his fists on his chest and then capture her mouth with his own, but first things first.

He grabbed the man holding Alivia and yanked him back, slamming his fist into his face, followed by an uppercut to the abdomen. The man was tough and would not go down easy. Good. With the intense need to protect Alivia surging through him, Klein wanted a battle.

Arms wrapped around his neck and one of the other men put him in a chokehold from behind. Klein grabbed at the guy's thick arms but couldn't dislodge him.

"Klein!" Alivia rushed toward him. The man in front of Klein whirled on her and wrapped her up tight, his arms staying securely around her even as she kicked and head-butted him.

The other man came from Klein's side as he continued to struggle unsuccessfully against the guy choking him. He saw the needle in the guy's hand before he grabbed Alivia's arm and plunged it in. Alivia kicked the guy and he grunted in pain, but Klein feared it was too late.

"No," he tried to holler, but it came out as nothing but a hoarse groan.

He pivoted and backed into the truck, trying to knock the man against the metal and off his back. Everything was going dark. He didn't know if it was the drugs they'd shot into him or the chokehold, but he felt himself sink to his knees with the man still clinging to him.

The blackness overwhelmed him, but the despair was worse.

He'd failed Alivia.

CHAPTER SEVEN

Alivia woke to a pounding headache, her hands zip tied behind her back, murky darkness surrounding her, a large, firm, and warm body pressed tight against her on one side, hard ground underneath, and taut vinyl on the other side.

She blinked, fighting the instinct to scream out and foolishly alert their captors she was awake.

It all came rushing back. Klein leaning in and maybe about to admit his feelings or even kiss her. The Navy men who'd attacked Thor and Shelly appearing and fighting with her and Klein.

Klein had been magnificent. He obviously wasn't a trained fighter like all the men in her family and the jerks who'd injected drugs into her and Klein and put a chokehold on Klein to win, but he had fought like a lion or a bear—or a man fighting for the love of his life.

She trembled at the memory. Something in his eyes had touched her deeply. He would've given his life for her. Maybe he cared for her as deeply as she did for him. And not just as a close friend or business partner, but as someone he could love. Was she making that up? Maybe. It had been an intense, surreal moment. She could be assigning emotion that wasn't there.

He had been about to say or do something incredible before those idiots showed up. Alivia had been distracted by all her dreams of Klein about to progress and hadn't heard the men approach until it had been too late. It was her fault they were in this mess. As soon as she got them free and got these Navy deserters arrested again, she would be brave enough to kiss Klein and see if they had a chance together. If he wasn't interested in happily ever after with her, she'd have to backtrack for the sake of their working relationship, but she prayed that wouldn't be the case. She wanted to throw caution to the wind and kiss him. For her, a kiss was everything, but maybe for a handsome thirty-year-old man who'd had women chasing him his entire life, a kiss might not have as much significance.

She pressed into his side and whispered, "Klein?"

He moved and let out a groan, but then his breathing settled again.

Crap. How was she going to wake him up and get their hands untied without alerting their captors? How much longer did she have until morning? Hopefully they were sleeping and not guarding them. If they were professionals, they'd have a guard posted, but she wasn't sure about these guys and their experience with kidnapping. Just because they could fight and were in the Navy didn't necessarily mean they were hardened criminals.

Would her family or Shelly realize they were missing yet? Shelly would hopefully notice when Klein didn't go home, but she might not, as wrapped up in Thor as she was. Even if she did notice, would she have any idea what job site Klein had been working at? Alivia lived alone and worked a lot of hours. She had days where she didn't see a family member, so it was likely nobody would miss her after one night. Double crap.

She pushed at Klein again. He didn't budge. She tried to get to the secret, padded pocket in her work pants that carried one of the small alloy knives Papa had gifted her for just such an occasion. She'd sown one into each of her work pants. Her phone, keys, and pocket knife were gone but she didn't think they'd discovered her hidden knife. She'd need Klein awake to get it out.

Her eyes had adjusted to the murky darkness. They were in a small, probably one-person tent. It made for tight quarters with a body as large as Klein's, and she wasn't some petite woman. It might've been romantic in any other situation, a small tent alone with the love of her life. If only she weren't so uncomfortable, he wasn't so unconscious, and they weren't in death's path.

She studied his handsome face, his dark curls, his irresistible lips. She loved the manly lines of his face and wished he'd open those green eyes and smile at her. As she stared at him, she could swear his features were getting more distinct. Was dawn approaching? Shoot. She needed to cut the zip ties off and get a jump on the three men before they stirred.

Even as she thought that, she heard movement, a tent zipper, and then footsteps.

She'd missed her chance.

"Klein," she whispered, pushing at him with her shoulder.

His eyelids fluttered and then opened. His eyes were unfocused, but he groaned, "Ali ..."

"Shh." She pressed harder against him and whispered into his neck, "Shh."

"Are you all right?" he whispered back. He sounded lucid, which was good.

"Yes. We need to get our hands free and then we can—"

"Rise and shine," a voice called from outside the tent. Their zipper went up and the tent flap was pulled open.

Klein scrambled onto his knees, pushed off with his feet, and plowed into the man. He led with his head and his shoulders like he was back in high school tackling the rival quarterback.

The man cried out in surprise as he slammed onto his back in the dirt.

She heard shouts from the other men and running steps.

Alivia crawled out of the tent to see Klein pinning the man to the ground. The other two men rushed up and one of them squatted next to her. She positioned herself to kick the legs out from under him, but froze when she felt cold steel jammed into the side of her neck. Without her hands secured, maybe she could find a way to best him, but she would be dead if she tried to fight right now.

"Hey, hero," the guy with the gun said. "Roll off of Colby and let's stop with the theatrics and the football tackles."

Klein whipped around to glower at the guy, looking like he was planning to tackle him next. His green eyes widened as he took in Alivia and the gun's position against her neck. "Ali."

He rolled off the other man, onto his knees, and stood. "Listen," he ground out. "I'll do anything you want. Just don't hurt her."

The look in Klein's green eyes hit Alivia down deep. He would do anything to keep her safe. Was that simply because he was an honorable man, or was she something special to him?

"Good to hear." The guy took Alivia's elbow and helped her to her feet but kept the gun pressed against her neck.

Alivia looked around, trying to get her bearings. They were in a thick forest. It looked like they were in the mountains close to home, but it could've been anywhere in Colorado. There were lots of pine, aspen, and juniper trees along with yellow, blue, red, and white wildflowers and thick undergrowth.

"Now, I think we should start over. I'm Travis." He gestured to his left at the guy flanking him. "That's Flynn." He nodded to the man struggling to his feet next to Klein. "And Colby. As Miss Delta knows, we were all ensigns in the Navy, but we opted for early retirement and are currently on a different assignment." He smirked at Alivia.

She stiffened and glared at him. "An assignment you're going to fail."

He pressed harder, and she winced as the gun dug into the tender skin of her neck.

"Watch it," Klein growled, starting forward.

"Don't, hero," Travis warned. "I don't want to kill her. It'll make my job harder, and I have personal issues with killing gorgeous blondes." His eyes narrowed and he held her tighter. "But I will do it if you give me any guff."

Klein stopped, looking torn in his need to defend her and yet not get her killed trying to be the hero.

"So, Klein and Ali?" Travis asked.

"Alivia," she bit out. No way was this loser using the nickname Klein had given her.

"Alivia." He raised his eyebrows but didn't seem to care what he called her. "Now here's the plan. We're going to have Alivia guide us straight to the weapon. Once it's in my possession, we'll tie you two up. I'm sure somebody will find you eventually." He looked directly at Klein and then at Alivia. "I won't kill either of you unless you force me to." He looked at his friends. "Flynn? Colby?"

"I don't want a gorgeous blonde's blood on my hands either." Flynn winked at Alivia. Klein let out a low growl, and Flynn edged away from him. "Just lead us to the weapon and then you two can get back to kissing."

Alivia rolled her eyes. If only it were that easy. She would protect the secret with her life, but how could she risk Klein's life for something he had no choice but to be part of? It was interesting how convinced these men were that the secret was a weapon. She'd assumed the same thing but wasn't certain. It could easily be a cure or a protection of some sort.

"I wouldn't mind killing him." Colby pointed at Klein as he rubbed his neck. "That's twice now he's knocked me into the dirt. But all I really want is the weapon, my paycheck, and relocation to some Southern Pacific island."

Alivia appreciated their promise not to kill them unless they had to. She didn't get the sense they were out for blood for the sake of blood. Hired mercenaries with a conscience. She hoped.

What she needed to know now was, "Who hired you?"

Travis smiled. "Oh, sweetheart. I'm sure your old man—"

"My grandpa," she corrected.

His eyebrows lifted. "He's fit."

Papa was more than "fit." He could take any of these men down.

"Your grandpa interrogated us, and none of us revealed our secrets to him. You think we'll spill them to you?"

She stared at him. She remembered Papa had been impressed and frustrated they hadn't revealed anything. "Admiral Seamons?"

Travis blinked at her. "You can guess all day and never figure it out, or we can get hiking and get our time together over with."

"You don't know who hired you, do you?" It was a stab in the dark, but something about him saying she could guess all day tipped her off.

His dark eyes widened slightly, but he recovered quickly. "Time to go."

"How can you trust them if you don't know who they are?"

"Because, sweetheart, they already paid us a million dollars and five more million is coming when I deliver the weapon."

It was a decent amount of money. She wished she had any idea who had hired them. "You're going to betray the country you've sworn to protect for a paycheck?"

He chuckled. "Don't try idealism with me. I've seen the way

your family lives. How do you know your beloved grandpa isn't a sellout? You think he's protecting the weapon for the good guys? Who are the good guys, Alivia? Do you have any idea how corrupt the U.S. government is?"

"Some may be corrupt, but many in the government and the military," she gave him a pointed look, "are honorable, good men and women trying to protect the freedoms and opportunity Americans enjoy that most of the world only dreams about." Even as she said the words, she knew that her family had been tasked to protect the secret because the creators knew corruption and greed happened too often in the government and whatever the secret was might prove too tempting to exploit or use for monetary gain. She also knew her family's success came from hard work, not some governmental payout like he was implying. The money Papa had been given to protect the secret had been used to build the cave, set up the security surrounding it, and provide the gold in the first cave that might trick some into thinking they'd found what they were after.

"Beautiful, feisty, and idealistic." He looked at Klein. "You're a lucky man. Or will be, if you both survive this." He smiled. "Sadly, we don't have time to stand around chatting. Flynn and Colby will pack up camp quick and then you can show us the way, beautiful."

The sky had lightened, and the sun was probably only twenty minutes from bursting over the mountains. Alivia forgot any desire to argue with this deserter in the face of needing to decide how to keep them from the secret's location and also protect Klein.

She could lead them to the cave; the fog and sensors would be activated and Papa and her family would come rescue her and Klein and arrest these three.

It sounded like a great option, but these three had already been bailed out of jail once and had someone wealthy and powerful backing them. They obviously had no idea where the secret was or they wouldn't risk a kidnapping. They weren't as smart as Lieutenant Moyle, who had utilized satellite pictures to get far too close to the cave. If she led these men close enough to the secret to set off the sensors, they might be able to make a better plan next time to bypass the sensors and cameras, or at least reveal the general location to whoever was paying them.

It might be an easier escape for her and Klein, but she couldn't do it. She said a prayer for help and then determined to lead them on a wild goose chase. She and Klein could escape, or Papa or her siblings or cousins would find them.

Flynn brought out protein bars and water bottles. He cut their zip ties. Alivia shook out her arms, rolled her shoulders, and flexed and extended her fingers. Before she could get too comfortable, or start formulating a plan now that her hands were free, Travis pulled out new zip ties and secured their hands in front.

"Thought I'd let you hike with your hands free?" Travis smirked at her.

She ignored him. He laughed and handed her two protein bars and a water bottle. She didn't want to take anything from them, but neither she nor Klein had eaten since yesterday at lunch and she planned to hike them all into the ground today. They ate and watched the other men quickly pack up the tents and their sleeping gear and shrug on huge backpacks.

"I need to use the bathroom," she said.

"All right," Travis said. "Flynn."

Flynn set down his backpack, pulled out a gun from his hip holster, and pointed it at Klein. Travis escorted her around some undergrowth and trees.

He took a couple steps back but stayed facing her with his gun pointed at her. "Go for it."

"You aren't watching me," she said.

"Yes, I am."

"Creep," Alivia muttered. She shuffled behind a thick pine tree and hurried to pee before he came after her. It was awkward undoing her zipper and pulling her pants down, but manageable.

Luckily, he just laughed at her. "Just try to run away. You know I'll kill Klein and then recapture you."

"I'm not running away," she hurled back. "But I'm not letting a pervert like you watch me pee."

"I've been very nice to you, Alivia," he said in a steely voice. "Don't upset me."

Alivia shuddered and hurried to finish and stride past him to the clearing. Klein watched her with concern. She tried to give him an encouraging smile, but it was shaky. She'd been prepared for a lot of things with her grandfather, parents, aunt and uncle training her and her cousins and siblings daily on weapons, fighting, self-defense, tracking, navigation, and other skills, but she never thought she'd be facing the enemy without the rest of her family as backup and with the man she loved as disposable collateral in the enemies' minds.

Travis shouldered a large backpack that was still half the size of Flynn and Colby's. The other two hefted their massive packs back on. Travis was obviously in charge, and the other two didn't seem to question that. He kept the gun on her the entire time. Klein kept catching her eye, but she didn't know what to convey to him. She tried to smile reassuringly. He probably had a million questions about what these guys were after and what the Delta family was hiding, but he said nothing.

Her wrists were aching and raw from the zip ties and her shoulders and back hurt from the way her arms had been secured behind her back last night and sleeping on the hard ground. At least their hands were secured in front of them, for now. Maybe she and Klein would get an opportunity to fight their way free or she could get to her knife with her hands in front of her.

"Lead the way, beautiful." Travis bowed to her.

Alivia had no idea where they were. There were mountain ranges surrounding the larger valley of Summit Valley and her family's smaller valley five miles east of town. Most of them looked exactly like where she was standing, and she wasn't an expert on navigation. She could find the cave if she left from her own home, but she wanted to keep them away from the cave. As she squinted around, she suddenly realized she did know where she was. That ridge to the west of them was where Klein had stood on Sunday evening while she'd been to the south of him. Relief filled her. If she went south, she could easily find the secret. She'd head northeast then.

She studied everything with a confident tilt to her chin, using the sun's angle to double check their location. Then, with one last glance at Klein, she pivoted and started toward a deer trail on the northeast side of the clearing.

"You know where you are?" Travis questioned from behind her. It sounded like he was either amazed or doubting her.

She gave him an imperious glare over her shoulder. "Of course I do. We're just southeast of the ski resort."

Travis's eyebrows went up. He looked impressed.

"The question is whether you can keep up." With that, she marched up the trail.

"Whew." One of the other men whistled. "She is smart and smoking hot."

"She's taken," Klein growled at him.

"She's still hot."

"Shut up," Travis told the guy.

Footsteps pounded behind her, and Alivia couldn't help but smile. They'd taken the bait. They thought she was leading them to the secret. She could lead them around these mountains for days and they'd all be desperately lost. Papa and her family would figure out something was wrong, and they'd find them. Her dad, Colt, and Greer were all incredible trackers. It would all be okay.

And Klein had said she was "taken." She wanted to sigh like a girlie girl. Maybe there was hope for the two of them. Now to keep them both alive until they could talk and she could finally get her first kiss with the man of her dreams.

CHAPTER EIGHT

Klein was a mess as he followed behind Flynn along the barely passable trail. Alivia led the way with Travis behind her, the pistol ever present in his hand and usually pointed at her back. Didn't the man's arm get tired? What if he tripped on a rock or some undergrowth? It was entirely too likely with this uneven trail and the fact they were all exhausted from hour after hour of hiking with little to no breaks for food and water. He might shoot her without even meaning to.

Colby took up the rear and kept reminding Klein that he'd better not try anything and saying how "hot" Alivia was until Klein thought he'd explode. He knew the man was trying to tick him off, but he didn't know how much more he could take. Unfortunately, Colby and Flynn also had sidearms or Klein might've had some hope they could escape.

The sun was dipping behind the trees at their backs, and Klein wished he could get a minute alone with Alivia. Where were they hiking to? Was she really leading them to some weapon? He'd always respected the Deltas and he knew Papa Delta was ex-military, but everybody in the valley thought he'd retired years ago. Whatever these thugs were after must be a well-protected military secret. He wondered which of the Deltas were involved. It sounded like Thor was and that was why these guys attacked him and Shelly. That made his gut churn. Was his sister in danger now? Would she be in danger in the future marrying a Delta? Did Shelly know? That didn't seem likely, or she would've told him. Right?

His mind was a mess of confusion, and he was worried about Alivia and about his grandma. Granny would be confused and upset when Klein didn't come home from work for the second night in a row. His legs ached from the long hike, his back hurt from sleeping on the ground, his shoulders, arms, and wrists hurt from being bound for so many hours, his head hurt from the hit with the crowbar, lack of sleep, the drugs, and lack of water.

He rolled his eyes at himself. He was whining like a child. At least it was all internal.

He glimpsed Alivia's trim form as she strode determinedly up the trail. She was hiking all of them into the dust. What an incredible woman she was. If only he could rescue her and love her. It seemed more likely at this point that she would rescue him. Where was this weapon? Alivia seemed unafraid as she led the way, but she knew exactly where they were. He was all turned around. If it wasn't for the sun slipping out of sight to the west, he'd have no idea what direction they were going. He should've paid more attention in scouts.

They reached a clearing with a small stream running through it. It would've been a picture-perfect spot if he and Alivia were alone. With these former military hired guns with them, it was hard to concentrate on any lush greenery and natural beauty.

"Stop," Travis commanded.

Alivia turned and Klein realized he was wrong. He could definitely concentrate on her natural beauty. Her hair had worked its way out of its standard ponytail and streamed around her face. Her smooth skin, blue eyes, and full pink lips called to him. She was dirty and disheveled, but she was the most gorgeous woman he'd ever seen.

"Are you leading us in circles?" Travis scowled at Alivia.

The mood in the clearing shifted. How in the world could Klein protect her without a weapon and only his strength to brag about? He didn't have military training like these guys, but he'd fight until they killed him.

Alivia tilted her chin imperiously. Despite her dirty, torn T-shirt and work pants, she had the bearing of a queen. "Have you been paying attention at all? We've been working our way north-northeast. How is that in circles?"

"Where is the weapon?" Travis yelled at her.

Klein eased around Flynn so he could tackle Travis if he tried anything. Flynn had slipped his huge backpack off and his head was down. He looked exhausted, and he didn't even seem to notice Klein's movement. Alivia and Klein had the disadvantage of crappy sleep, drugs in their system, hands zip tied, and no dinner last night, but Flynn and Colby were carrying packs that probably weighed over fifty pounds each.

"It's at least a two-day hike," she said. "If you all could pick up the pace, we can be there tomorrow before dark."

"Why didn't you tell me that this morning?"

"You didn't ask," she said in a falsely sweet tone.

Travis growled, and Klein's hackles rose.

"We'll have to camp here," he spat out. "Flynn, Colby. Set everything up before we run out of daylight. I'll feed these two, then we can zip tie their hands behind their backs and shove them in the tent. Let them rest peacefully so we can get to the weapon tomorrow." He glared at Alivia. "You'd better not be leading us astray. If we don't get to the weapon by tomorrow before dark, I'll kill him."

Klein felt pinpricks of danger. Would Travis really kill him?

"I just told you it was at least a two-day hike," she flung back at Travis. "We might not make it before tomorrow at dark. And you will not kill him, or I won't lead you any further and you'll never get your stupid weapon." Alivia wasn't yelling, but her voice was very loud and very much in control.

Travis looked stumped, but then his dark eyes got a gleam in them. "You're right. Killing him won't work, at least not yet." His jaw tightened. "If we are not to the weapon by tomorrow at dark, I will shoot him in the shoulder. Repeatedly. Until I'm sure a few bullets are lodged in all that muscle. Those bullets will fester. He'll be in a lot of pain, and we'll leave him behind. Then you will take us to the weapon, after which we will release you and you can find your man again. If he hasn't bled to death or been attacked by a mountain lion or bear at that point. It's not likely you'll be able to get him the help he needs even if you do get back to him, unless you get us there quickly." He gave her a significant look. "Get us there."

Then he whirled and stomped to the pack that Flynn was taking sleeping gear out of and started ripping out empty water bottles to fill in the stream. Colby had the tents out of his pack and was setting each one up.

Klein met Alivia's gaze. She had looked so proud and so in control, but now she looked terrified. She looked like Travis was going to fulfill his threat and Klein was going to get shot in the shoulder multiple times tomorrow evening and be left to die. It wasn't a given that he'd get an infection, but he might bleed to death or be attacked by animals. He didn't relish the idea of getting shot, but it warmed his heart that Alivia seemed so concerned.

He tried to smile to reassure her. "It'll be all right."

He heard Travis mutter something angrily at the stream.

Alivia turned away. Klein was so impressed with her. Despite the discomfort and worry that Travis would accidentally shoot Alivia, Klein believed heaven was on their side. He hadn't stopped praying for heavenly protection and guidance. It would all work out. Somehow.

Or maybe not. That look of horror in Alivia's gaze and her lack of response to Travis's threat boded very badly for him.

Would they get to the weapon by tomorrow evening? What other options did Alivia have? All the questions about the weapon, the Deltas, how Granny and Shelly were faring, how many emergencies were erupting at work, and most importantly if Alivia could love him, seemed far away as Klein felt Alivia's despair and fears as if they were his own.

CHAPTER NINE

Alivia was panicking as they finished their meager dinner, used the bathroom, and had their hands cut loose and then zip tied behind their backs. She'd gambled with Klein's life by deciding to lead these idiots on a wild goose chase instead of leading them to the cave and relying on the sensors and fog to get these guys recaptured. She still thought it was logically smarter not to let them know where the secret was and let that information get out, but she also knew that tomorrow night Travis would shoot Klein in the shoulder. Repeatedly. Then leave him to die.

She didn't believe Travis was a cold-blooded murderer, but he would follow through on his threat. It was like the time as a teenager that she and Thor had stolen dynamite from a farmer in a valley thirty miles away and blown up several dumpsters. They'd never been caught, but her mom had known it was her. She always knew. She'd threatened to ground Alivia from her truck for a year if she did anything like that again. Alivia had laughed at the extravagant threat that she knew her mom would never follow through with, as Colt had already left for college and Mom would've had to drive Alivia and her sisters everywhere. Her mom's eyes had narrowed, and she'd told her she'd take her laptop with her home drafting program and lock it in the safe for three months. Alivia had known that threat would happen, and she'd toed the line.

It was the same with Travis. He didn't want to kill Klein, and he might not follow through with that particular threat, but he would definitely shoot him in the shoulder. She'd seen the proof of that in his cold, dark gaze.

If Klein got shot, he could bleed to death, be attacked by an animal who smelled the blood, or get an infection and die before she could get back to him and then get him to help. There was also the worry that Travis would miss and hit a vital organ or Klein's heart.

The other problem was that Alivia had led them far away from the secret. She could hike that direction all day tomorrow and Travis would definitely know she'd led him in the opposite direction, but they would still be farther than a half-day's hike from the secret and Klein would be in big trouble. Even if they escaped, she couldn't have Klein weakened by gunshot wounds and a possible infection and somehow get away from these three and find their way to help and get these jerks arrested.

Had she made a mistake? She'd been cocky to think she could lead them astray and not face the consequences. She might have protected the secret's location, but she had jeopardized Klein's life.

There was only one option. They had to get free. Tonight.

She and Klein got escorted to and zipped into the small tent. The sun was long gone, and it was dark. Klein's firm chest brushed against her as they both crouched in the small space.

"Let's kneel first. Then we can figure out how to lie down and get comfortable," he said.

She leaned in close and found her lips pressed against his neck.

A tremor went through her that she fought to ignore. "Let's lie down with your back to my front so you can get my knife."

"They didn't take your knife?" His warm breath brushed her forehead. They both always carried pocketknives, but she was certain her secret knife was still there.

"I have a secret compartment in all my pants," she whispered back. "Go through the pocket on my right thigh and then you should be able to rip the material and find the knife."

"You're amazing."

She smiled, loving his sincere words. It was the first time she'd felt reassured all day.

They both kneeled and then lay down with his back to her front, squirming around until she finally felt his hands pressing against her right thigh where the pocket was. Klein would never be a grabby-hands type of guy, but with his hands brushing her leg repeatedly, thrills shot through her.

She wanted to talk to him, tell him so many things, and ask how he was feeling and what he was thinking about her, about this weapon Travis was after, if he was mad at her for putting him in danger, how their families and employees were dealing with their disappearance, the list could go on, but getting free was the priority.

With him facing away and sliding down low so he could access her pocket, she couldn't exactly whisper into his neck like she had earlier. Oh my, that had felt good.

She shook her head. She was so miserable every which way that she had to be exaggerating how good it had felt.

Or maybe not. His hands brushed her leg as he tried to gently rip the lining of the pocket. She shivered.

"Are you cold?" Klein asked softly.

"I'm okay," she managed.

A few seconds of silence passed. She could hear Klein's

breathing as he fumbled with his hands secured and tried to rip open the material quietly. She could hear somebody else's breathing as well. How close were those jerks sleeping to them?

"Can you tell me about this weapon they're after?"

"I can't talk about it," she muttered.

Klein let out a heavy breath. "Will we get there tomorrow night?"

Alivia had no idea how to answer. Could she admit to him that she'd led them astray and there was no way would they get there by tomorrow night? She'd gambled and he would be the one to lose. Travis and the others would probably hear anything she said, though, so she said nothing.

"Come on, Alivia," a voice said from outside the tent. "I want to know more about the weapon, too."

It was Colby. Could he hear Klein's movements as he finally succeeded in ripping the lining and slid the small, flat knife out? Maybe she should talk to cover the sound.

"What do you want?" she asked, while slowly rolling over so her zip ties were accessible to Klein.

"I'm right outside your tent," Colby said. "I'll be here half the night, then Flynn will take my spot. If you need a real man to keep you warm, just say the word, pretty girl."

"If you want me to tackle you so hard you'll never stand up or speak again, keep talking right now," Klein threatened as he flipped open the small knife and started sawing at her zip ties.

Colby laughed shortly. "You're a big threat, tool guy. I'm trained as a lethal weapon. You're trained to hammer nails into walls like a hack."

"I don't need training to take out a wimp like you," Klein said.

"You won't need anything when I'm through with you," Colby shot back. "But your girlfriend is going to need a new man soon, and I'll be right here waiting for her."

Alivia wanted to yell at them to stop. What if Colby fulfilled his threats? But the knife made a scraping sound as Klein tried to cut through or pop open the zip ties with his hands in an awkward position behind his back and only the small knife to assist him.

"You'll never touch Alivia," Klein said. "Let me loose and we'll see who the real man is."

Alivia felt flushed from the protectiveness in his tone, but she needed them to both calm down so a miracle would happen and Colby would fall asleep from exhaustion and boredom, not be stirred up in anger and try to fight Klein. She'd love to thrash any of these men, but they had to keep their heads and escape while they slept.

"Klein," she warned softly.

"You want to go?" Colby yelled over her. She could hear him scrambling to his knees.

Oh, crap.

"Everybody's tired," Alivia tried. "Let's just calm down."

"Colby!" Travis's voice cracked through the night. "Stop acting like a hopped-up-on-steroids idiot and let us get some sleep, or I'll make you guard them all night long."

A tense silence filled the area. Alivia could feel Klein shaking as he sawed at her restraints. She hoped he didn't cut her wrist or his own fingers. He was furious. He would probably thrash Colby if Colby let him loose, but that wouldn't help them escape.

"Klein," she whispered softly.

He stopped sawing. Alivia cautiously touched Klein's clenched left fist and gently rubbed at his tight skin. She felt him relax under her touch.

"Fine," Colby bit out.

Alivia heard him settle back down on the mat or whatever he had in front of their door. Thankfully, Travis had stopped him. She wasn't sure what Klein was thinking. If these men would fall asleep, and they could get their zip ties off, they might have a chance to escape tonight. If Colby had opened the tent and seen their position and that Klein had a knife working on her zip ties, it could've messed up everything. At the same time, she couldn't help but love Klein even more for wanting to defend her.

Klein's hands relaxed, and he threaded the fingers of his free hand together with hers. Her heart raced for a completely different reason than the fear she'd felt today and the concern of a moment ago. Ah, Klein. How could a simple touch make her feel warm, tingly, and like she was the most important person in the world to him?

She wanted to roll over and kiss him, but she had to let him focus and cut her bonds. His life was more important than her selfish desires. She listened to the sound of Travis or Flynn getting settled in the nearest tent. She prayed these men would fall asleep and be heavy sleepers or no way were they getting out of here. They had hiked a long distance today with heavy backpacks on. Even though Travis's backpack was smaller than the other two, she suspected it had some serious weapons in it from the bulges she'd seen.

Releasing her hand from his, she felt Klein pull on the plastic with his left hand while sawing with his right.

The minutes ticked slowly by, and she heard a soft pop as the zip tie finally broke. She wanted to cheer. Klein squeezed her hand and handed off the knife, handle first. They both rolled over. In the quiet night, the sound of vinyl crackling seemed as loud as a gunshot.

"Sorry," Klein said. "Just wanted to get as close as possible."

She didn't mind him close. She'd never felt anything so thrilling. It was also a great excuse for the sound.

Colby gave a disgusted grunt outside of the tent, but he said nothing. Dang. He was still awake. She kept praying that he'd fall asleep. He had to be exhausted and probably thought they had no means to get free. From the sound of it, he was lying on a cot in front of the door. It would be a miracle to get over him without waking him, but if he didn't even go to sleep they'd really be in trouble.

She started sawing at Klein's restraints and prayed she could get him free. She also prayed Colby wouldn't hear the quiet scratching sound it made as she worked. She didn't want him to figure out what they were doing or poke his head in to investigate.

"Tell me about ... Granny," she softly requested. If she could get Klein talking about something these men wouldn't care about, it would cover any noise. It might also lull Colby to sleep if he thought it was boring enough. Or it might annoy him and keep him awake. She'd keep talking until Klein's zip ties were off, then reevaluate.

"Granny's a sweetie," Klein said, the love in his voice obvious. "I'm worried it'll be hard on her not knowing where I am and if I'm okay."

"Poor baby boy," Colby taunted from outside the tent.

Klein stiffened.

"Ignore him," Alivia said. "Is it working out okay with the nurses coming in to take care of her?" She didn't want to hear about how great Kelsey was, but she was scrambling to cover the noise of her cutting off his ties. The knife was small, but it had worked on her zip ties, so it should work on his.

"It's all right. She loves them both, but the doctors keep pushing us to get her in a care facility where they have around-the-clock care, therapists who could work with her every weekday instead of when we take her in, and dietitians who would make sure her diet was the best possible to slow the progress of the disease. Shelly and I hate to have her not with us, and the facility is in Denver and crazy expensive ..."

Klein kept talking, telling her about Granny's symptoms of memory loss, confusion, losing balance, repeating questions, taking a long time to complete any task, and sometimes even hallucinating and telling them his dad or his grandpa were right there in the room.

He told her about the medications they had Granny taking, the myriad of foods they tried that could combat dementia, and the occupational therapists and doctors they went to see. Sadly, none of it seemed to be reversing the effects but hopefully slowed them. Of course her nurses Wendy and Kelsey were incredible and a blessing for the family. Mo was adorable. Alivia agreed. She just hoped Klein didn't realize what a perfect catch Kelsey was. She could only imagine how a sweet young mom like Kelsey would yearn for an amazing man like Klein to be there for her and her son.

The zip tie finally popped free, distracting her from the Kelsey situation. She wanted to scream happily. Instead, she kept asking Klein questions.

They talked about Shelly and Thor and then talked through each of the homes they were building, the issues with each one and the worries of the men falling behind without them. It bothered her not to be working and she hated to not hit a deadline, but there was nothing she could do about it. She and Klein had to escape first.

It was at least another hour before she slowly made her way to her knees. Klein followed, their voices hopefully muffling the sound of their movements.

In the same tone of voice that she'd been discussing Granny and her care, their construction work, and Thor and Shelly, she said, "Do you think Colby is a pathetic loser, or is it just me?" She was hoping to see if Colby was awake, but then she realized her question might tick him off and mess everything up.

"No, I agree one hundred percent. Colby is a waste of military talent, wouldn't know loyalty if it bit him on the butt, and couldn't fight his way out of a paper bag."

Either Colby would rip the tent open and their gig would be up, or his non response would show he was asleep. If he was awake and got angry, they could try to overpower him and make a run for it before the others pursued. She'd much rather sneak away quietly.

"I actually prefer plastic bags for my groceries, but I'm sure that's not the best for recycling." She was talking nonsense now, but she wanted to keep their conversation going and hopefully if anybody was awake, they'd just hear their voices and not the zipper as she slowly slid it up.

"I'm not sure about the recycling," Klein said amicably. "I'd have to agree with you, though. You can carry a bunch of bags easier and they don't rip through."

"Good point." The zipper was up, and she slowly swept the material to the side. "I'm sure you can carry lots of bags with those muscles."

She paused and looked out. Colby was sprawled out on a mat in front of her, his mouth slightly open and his eyes closed. He must've been exhausted from carrying that pack all day, and the sound of their voices had lulled him to sleep. Colby had failed at guard duty. Praise heaven above.

The silence was eerie, but she could hear his even breathing. She didn't dare move as she strained to listen for a movement from one of the other tents set up close to their own.

Glancing back at Klein, she gestured out with her head. He nodded. She eased to her feet, crouching, and bent in half. Klein eased closer, crouching as well. He held the tent flap for her.

She studied Colby, trying to gauge where to step so she didn't step on him by accident and wake him up. Slowly easing to the left, she placed her right foot outside the tent on the small spot of dirt between the tent and Colby's mat. She straightened out of the opening and lifted her left foot out. Leaning to the left, she needed to clear Colby's legs. She swayed and fear rolled through her. She could not get off balance and fall straight onto Colby.

Klein's hand on her elbow steadied and reassured her. With him as an anchor, she could reach her left foot out far enough to clear Colby's long legs, then push off of Klein. She was squatting at the far end of Colby's mat. She inched back, straightening, and turned to offer Klein a hand. He placed his right foot just outside the tent, took her hand, and jumped over Colby.

Klein landed right in front of her, pressing into her and wrapping his arms around her for stability. Alivia gasped, hoping Klein's landing didn't wake any of the men. They froze, staring down at Colby, but also listening for any movement in the tents.

Crickets chirped, an owl softly hooted, wind rustled the trees, and her own heart beat out of control. Was it Klein being so close or the risk of being caught? Honestly, she thought it might be all Klein's warm strength pressing into her.

She looked up at him. It was dark, with only a sliver of moon that barely poked its light through the thick pines. She could make out his features and see him nod slightly. All she wanted was to lean in and kiss him, but she had to think like a Delta and not a woman desperate to kiss a man. They hadn't been discovered yet, and they needed to move. Pronto.

She snapped out of her Klein-induced daze and backed slowly away from him. Twisting, she reached over and gently slid the zipper back into place. Then she started across the camp. The moon had just risen to the east, so she aimed for a southwest angle to get them back to their valley. She couldn't afford to second guess herself, but she remembered Papa telling them how the moon could have different positioning depending on its cycle, the time of year, or its fullness. Shoot. What if this was one of those times it didn't raise straight to the east?

She heard a rustle behind her and looked back. Klein lifted both of the large backpacks up and slung one over each shoulder. He strode to her, and she tried to reach for one. He shook his head and pointed forward.

Alivia always carried her own weight, and it frustrated her that he wouldn't let her carry a backpack, but now was not the time to argue about it. She headed through the trees, cautiously feeling her way along the semi-broken deer trail they'd trudged up earlier.

Would she be able to get them home, or would she get them completely lost? Anything was better than being near Travis, Flynn, and Colby, but she wanted to finish this. If only she could get her and Klein safe and get these guys captured. She didn't want them going after anyone else in her family in their quest to find the secret. They were only in it for the money, but the fact was somebody had offered six million dollars to get what they all thought was a weapon. Who was it? How would this affect her family? They'd all known there was a possibility they'd have to up their protection of the secret and maybe even call everyone home and put their own careers on hold for a time.

They hadn't gone a hundred yards when Klein stopped her with a hand on her back and her thoughts scattered. She turned back to him. He held up a hand, then set both backpacks on the ground. With the tents, sleeping mats, and a lot of the food gone, they were both much lighter.

Rifling through the one, he pulled out a flashlight and handed it to her. They were far enough away now that she could click it on. She did, and Klein gestured to the first backpack. She pointed the flashlight into it. He quickly removed any food, refillable water bottles, a couple of knives, a gun, a box of bullets, and a first aid kit and put them in the other backpack. He pulled out a compass and handed it to her.

"This would've been helpful this morning," she whispered.

He smiled. Strapping the fuller backpack on, he hid the other one behind some underbrush, then gestured for her to keep going. That was smart. Without the sleeping gear, they didn't need both backpacks and could take turns carrying this one.

Alivia was happy to have the flashlight. She held it up to the compass, determined the best path was the trail they'd come in on, and started plodding along the trail that meandered but led mostly southwest.

Neither of them spoke as they trudged along the trail that had been broken by animals over the years but deepened by them going the other direction with the men earlier today. Her blisters probably had blisters. She hadn't dared take her shoes off last night, knowing they would need to be ready to run, but now she'd give anything to get them off.

A stream trickled by up ahead. They stopped to get a drink and refill a couple water bottles.

"Do you want me to carry the pack?" she asked.

"No thank you," Klein said.

Alivia took a deep breath in and out rather than telling him to stop. He was being a gentleman and she was grateful for that, but he had to be as tired as she was.

"How are you holding up?" Klein asked.

"Tired, but we need to keep going. We have to get more distance from them."

He nodded. "Okay."

She straightened, pointed the flashlight at the compass, and started off again. Alivia concentrated on going the right direction, which wasn't easy as the trail meandered, and somehow putting one foot in front of the other. How long could they keep going? Should they hunker down and sleep for a few hours? How much distance had they put between themselves and the men? Not enough, but what would be enough? Her biggest hope was Papa, her dad, or someone from her family would find them. They had to be looking. Even if Shelly hadn't discovered that Klein hadn't come home the night before, one of their workers would've discovered both of their trucks, tried to call their phones, and sounded the alarm this morning.

She stumbled and Klein steadied her with a hand on her elbow. He drew her against his chest, and she let him. She couldn't wrap her arms around him with the huge backpack on, so she simply burrowed her head into the crook of his neck and let him hold her. She needed him, his solid strength, comfort, and the reassurance that he was here by her side.

"You need to rest," he said softly.

"I'm afraid they'll find us."

"It's okay to be afraid, but now we've got weapons and can fight them if they come. Come on, Ali. Let's find a spot to lie down off this trail, then I'll come back and cover our tracks."

"You know how to cover tracks?" she asked. Did he not realize that Travis had a lot more weapons than the one pistol they'd found in the backpack?

He chuckled. "I'm obviously not a Delta trained fighter, but I can figure out how to brush off our prints with a pine bough or something."

Alivia should've argued for them to keep moving. She could hope Travis didn't even know they were gone yet, but it was probably past time for Flynn and Colby to change guard duty. Maybe they wouldn't even check on them or listen for their breathing. She didn't know if they could be so lucky, but she did know they were both exhausted. They had to get some sleep so they could hopefully hike out of here tomorrow.

They searched away from the trail for a spot they could conceal themselves. Her flashlight illuminated a spot of pine trees and undergrowth she would've loved to pretend was a small fort as a child. They could both crawl into it and lay down, but it would also provide coverage from anyone looking for them.

Klein leaned into the spot and spread the blanket out from the pack. Alivia climbed in first and sat down on it. He handed over a water bottle and a pack of trail mix. "Eat and I'll be back."

Alivia watched the flashlight bob away. She should be more concerned about some animal coming in here, or the men being after them, but she was simply too tired. She was scared too, maybe irrationally so. She wanted Klein back by her side. Her mind was foggy with fear, exhaustion, and uncertainty. The only hope she could find in this dark spot was Klein. She needed to focus on heavenly hope, not trust in a man, but oh what a man he was.

She munched on the trail mix, pushed away her yearning for Klein, and prayed desperately. *Please protect us. Please send help.*

She saw the light coming back and breathed a sigh of relief. Klein burrowed into the hiding spot and she got a glimpse of his handsome face before he focused the light on the backpack and got his own trail mix and water.

He turned the flashlight off and stowed it in the backpack while they both munched. She finished, shoving her garbage in a pocket of the backpack, and took a long drink of water. There were so many things to say to him, but she had no idea where to start.

He finished his snack, put his garbage in the side pocket, took their water bottles and zipped them into the backpack, then said, "Before we lie down, do you want to pray together?"

Alivia sucked in a breath. Was it any wonder she thought he was perfect? "I would love that."

They kneeled together, clasped hands, and he asked, "Do you want me to offer it?"

"Yes, please."

He cleared his throat, then began. "Dear Father. We thank thee for protecting us and making it possible for us to escape. Please watch over us as we rest. Please return us safely to our families. Please bless, if possible, that help can come and Travis, Flynn, and Colby can be captured so they will not threaten or hurt the Delta family, Shelly, or Granny in any way. We love thee and we're grateful for our friendship. In the name of our Savior, amen."

"Amen," Alivia repeated, awed by the strength of faith and testimony she felt more than heard from him. She felt more at peace than she had since the men had appeared and interrupted what might've been their first kiss last night. Her first kiss ever. She'd wanted that kiss so badly.

She needed to stop thinking about kissing.

"Thank you," she said to Klein, hoping he couldn't read in her voice that her thoughts had shifted quickly from his meaningful prayer to her longing to kiss him.

"Of course." She heard him slide down on the emergency blanket.

She lay next to him, accidentally far too close, but in her defense there wasn't much room between the scratchy branches of the pine tree.

Klein shifted, slid his arm beneath her back, and turned her into his side. The mood instantly shifted, and she was hyper-aware of every spot of their bodies that seemed fused together. A tremor rippled through her born of warmth, excitement, and the feeling that she was where she'd always been meant to be.

"Is that comfortable for you?" he asked with a husky tone to his voice that she loved.

"Um ..."

Comfortable? She was miles past comfortable. She laid her head against his muscular chest and loved that he smelled like the out of doors and pine needles. She worried what she smelled like but was too tired and exhilarated at the same time to care.

"Is it not comfortable for you?" His voice was more reluctant.

"I definitely won't fall asleep like this."

He started to release her.

"Don't you dare let me go," Alivia said fiercely.

"Oh, okay." His arms tightened around her again.

"It's probably just the exhaustion talking, so don't hold this against me in the morning, but ..." She tried to make herself stop, but found she didn't want to. They might not survive the night. What did it matter if she begged him to kiss her? "I've never loved being exhausted, dirty, probably stinky, in danger, and lying on the hard ground so much. I love your arms around me."

He chuckled softly. "I won't hold it against you. Holding you in my arms is a slice of heaven I've prayed for most of my adult life."

Alivia's eyes widened. She wanted to ask if he was serious, but she didn't know that she should open up a discussion about what he'd meant by that. She was too out of it, too tired, too stressed. Her actions had led him here, and she didn't want to put him in more danger because of her lack of self-control right now, but kissing him was at the forefront of her mind and she found she couldn't resist telling him that.

"Klein, can I tell you a really embarrassing secret?" She should shut her mouth right now. This was like the tent at girls' camp where you said things in the comfortable darkness you'd regret in the morning. Instead of being in her own sleeping bag, she was in the arms of the most beautiful and desirable man on the planet.

"You can tell me anything."

It was much easier without being able to see his handsome face. Without being able to see the surprise in those green eyes. "I've never been kissed."

"What?" He jumped and must've smacked his head on a branch above them. "Ouch." He settled back down and held tighter to her. "What kind of idiots did you date in high school?"

"I never really dated in high school. Or after," she admitted. "Too much of a tomboy, I guess."

She felt Klein's head shake. "Ali ... You might not wear a bunch of makeup, but there's nothing boyish about you. Anyone can see you're the perfect combination of tough and feminine."

She loved that he saw her like that.

"Other boys and men must've been intimidated by you. I know I have been."

"You have?"

"For sure. You're so impressive. It's hard to think I could be worthy of you."

Alivia wanted to gush that he was more than worthy of her, but he kept going.

"Any man would want to date and kiss a woman as smart, kind, fun, hard-working, and irresistibly beautiful as you."

Alivia's heart sped up. She wished she could record all these beautiful words so she'd never forget them. Her right arm was trapped between their bodies, but her left hand moved of its own volition, running along his shoulder, across his neck, and cupping his bearded jaw. Klein moaned softly, and she felt empowered by that moan and his words, reckless because she was tired and in danger, but overshadowing everything was how deeply she loved him.

"Would you want to date and kiss me, Klein?" She didn't know if it was the right question, but she was an infant when it came to emotional connection with men and especially with this most important man to her. She needed the reassurance.

"Oh, Ali ..." Klein's arms tightened around her. "Would I ever."

He said nothing else. He simply pressed his lips to hers.

Ali's breath caught and her heart thudded out of control. His kiss was soft and tender and didn't ask anything of her. It simply showed her how beautiful a sweet touching of the mouths could be, like two souls touching heart to heart.

One of his hands slowly made its way up her back and his fingers threaded into her hair. He drew back slightly, their breath intermingling and her desire for him growing. He came in again. This time his lips moved against hers and she was overwhelmed by the tingling sensation that erupted in her lips.

Alivia had no idea what she was doing, but her mouth seemed to need no training. She'd worked for years to perfect her fighting and construction skills. Kissing Klein wasn't work at all. It was easy and beautiful.

Her lips moved in synchrony with his. The kisses slowly became more intricate, more intense, more tingly, more consuming. She forgot every worry she'd ever had as she felt more alive, vibrant, and desirable in Klein's arms, with his mouth working its magic on her, than she'd ever felt in her life.

She had no clue how long they kissed, and she didn't much care. She could die right now and her life would be complete.

Klein slowed the kisses down and held her close. She waited and hoped for more sweet words from him, but as her eyelids fluttered open to stare into his green eyes, she realized ... she not only could see his green eyes, but she could see his entire handsome face. The night was lightening around them and dawn was probably half an hour away. They'd probably kissed for over an hour. She wouldn't complain about the kissing, but she should've exercised more self-control.

"Oh, Klein, I'm sorry. We just kissed away the time we should've been resting."

"Don't apologize for those kisses." He smiled. "With kisses like that, I won't need sleep to energize me."

Alivia's heart thumped harder, and she wanted to kiss him all over again. "Is all kissing that incredible?" she asked, suddenly uncertain if she'd even done it right. She'd been so consumed by him that she hadn't stopped to worry.

"No." He shook his head. "I've never experienced kissing like that before."

Alivia's breath caught and then rushed out. She wanted to tell him she loved him. Instead, she pressed her lips to his again. The kiss took on a life of its own and she was lost in the sweet ecstasy that was Klein Vance. Who knew her business partner would be the perfect fit for her mouth and for her? She'd wondered, and now she had her answer. How would they go about navigating a relationship from here? Who cared right now? She only wanted to keep kissing.

A loud rustling noise penetrated through the fog of happy kissing. Alivia drew back and saw Klein had an identical concerned expression. She closed her eyes so she could ascertain if it was human or animal. Her gut churned with horror knowing they'd been discovered. She'd been distracted by kissing Klein, and not only had she used up the time they should've been sleeping so they could make it home safe, but now she'd endangered both of them.

It sounded like the shuffling of an animal dragging something. Would the animal pass them by? She prayed for help and immediately felt the impression. "Move," she whispered harshly to Klein.

He nodded, scrambled up to a crouch, grabbed the backpack, and edged out of their hiding spot. She quickly followed just in time to see a large mountain lion dragging half a deer carcass right at them. Oh, crap. They'd been in his spot.

Klein tugged her away from the opening. The lion released the deer from its jaws, let out a spine-tingling snarl, and sprung at them.

Klein jumped in front of Alivia, swinging the heavy backpack at the lion. Alivia screamed. The backpack connected with the lion's head and shoulders and deflected it into a pine tree.

"Run," Klein yelled.

Alivia turned and sprinted through the thick undergrowth. Klein was right at her heels. The lion seemed stunned, and for a few seconds she didn't hear any pursuit. She dared to hope the animal wouldn't chase them. She knew they shouldn't run from a mountain lion. Her dad had taught her to turn and face the animal, back away slowly, make herself look bigger, yell and maybe throw things, but the need to run was overwhelming. She prayed desperately and felt her legs move faster. That confirmed it wasn't just the natural instinct to flee.

She reached the trail they'd walked yesterday afternoon with their captors and early this morning to escape. The mountain lion crashed through the brush in pursuit. Crying out, she tried to go faster. Her legs were tired, but she felt like she had heavenly strength. She could swear she heard footsteps coming toward them and thought she saw a flash of bright blue through the trees.

Would more humans be able to help them, or would it be Travis, Colby, and Flynn? Those three were a worse option than a mountain lion.

She looked back and could see directly over Klein's shoulder that the mountain lion was almost upon them. Turning forward, she saw Flynn round the corner first with the other two right behind him.

"Yes!" he yelled, running in their direction and pulling his pistol from his hip holster.

Alivia had no idea what to do now. Cold prickles enveloped her body.

"Ali," Klein called, then tackled her from behind. He wrapped her up and prevented her from slamming face-first into the ground, but the impact of his heavy body on top of hers hurt.

The mountain lion flew over the top of them and collided with Flynn with a horrifying snarl.

Klein jumped to his feet, pulling Alivia up with him. They

turned and sprinted the other direction. Alivia could hear shouts and cries of pain and a battle raging behind them. She ignored any pain and concentrated on running faster than she ever had the other direction.

She hated to hope the mountain lion won, but she'd rather fight a mountain lion than be in those men's power again.

Where are you, Papa?

As she ran, she was reassured by Klein keeping pace with her and the sounds of the battle fading behind them. When several gunshots rang out, she feared the men had won. How soon would they catch up?

She prayed desperately for help and safe shelter.

CHAPTER TEN

Klein followed Alivia down the narrow trail. He had no idea if they were going the right direction. The only feeling he had was to keep moving as fast as they could. He did have a gun and bullets now, but Flynn, Colby, and Travis were all armed and a lot better trained than he was. Alivia was probably better trained than he was. He'd wanted to ask her so many questions. Instead, they'd kissed away the hour they should've rested. He didn't regret it at all.

He loved her. How soon could he tell her that without scaring her away?

His legs were shaky and each pounding step shot pain up his spine. The backpack dug viciously into his shoulders, but he couldn't dump it and lose the gun and bullets. No way could they slow down or stop. How far away were they from civilization, from help? Would her family be tracking them? Sheriff Reed? How would anybody even know where they'd gone? Klein didn't even know how far away they'd hiked yesterday and there were a lot of mountains surrounding their valley.

He strained to listen but wasn't sure if it was their pursuers' footsteps behind them, or if it was all the pounding of his and Alivia's footfalls. As hard as they were running, and as scared as he was, it could be the pounding of his own heart. He could hardly catch a full breath and had no idea how much longer they could keep going.

Alivia looked back over her shoulder at him. He tried to smile to reassure her, but it probably looked like a grimace.

She suddenly cried out, flew forward, then dropped onto one knee. Klein barely stopped himself from plowing her over.

"You okay?" he rasped out, reaching his hand under her shoulder to help her up.

"My ankle," she said. She pointed back up the trail. "I stepped on that boulder and it snapped to the side."

Oh, please no. He tried not to show the distress in his face, but this was horrific. He listened and sure enough, he could hear footsteps in the distance. If only he could judge how far they were away and if they had any time to hide. Where could they hide?

Alivia let him help her up. She tried to put pressure on her left ankle and winced. "Let's go," she muttered, hobbling forward.

Klein put his arm around her and they half-ran along the trail. The sounds of pursuit were getting louder and louder. Neither of them spoke. What was there to say? Trained, furious, ex-military mercenaries were behind them and gaining fast. They might keep Alivia alive to lead them to the weapon, but who knew? They might be angry enough to kill them both on sight.

They wouldn't take Alivia from him without a battle. Klein was strong, but he had no idea how to win against three armed and experienced men. Should he stop and make a stand? Should he keep pushing forward and hope for some help?

Klein couldn't think when he'd felt such sheer terror in his life, but right now he could taste it, smell it, feel it. He prayed desperately and something urged him to veer Alivia off the trail to the right. "This way."

She looked at him like she wasn't certain if going off the trail was smart, but she limped along as he tried to support her over rocks and roots and around the larger bushes. He didn't even know what to hope for. If they could get off the trail far enough, could the men somehow pass them by? Should they hide behind a bush, get the pistol and knives ready, and pray they could hold them off? Hold them off until what? They had no idea if anybody could find them or even if her family or the sheriff's department was looking.

He kept pushing the direction he felt they should go. The early morning sun strained to peek through the dense trees. It was straight behind him, so he was heading west.

"What are you thinking?" Alivia murmured.

"I'm not," he admitted. "Just praying and feeling."

She arched an eyebrow but didn't comment. They kept moving. Those footsteps on the trail just beyond them grew louder. The men were close. Every second they gained on them. Those footsteps were a death march. Klein glanced around but couldn't see anyone through the thick trees. Could they hear him and Alivia? There was no way to outrun them with Alivia hurt.

Please help, he begged heaven above.

Alivia let out a quick gasp of air and pointed through the trees. "Klein."

What now? A bear or moose to finish them off? Maybe a pack of wolves. At least they'd die together. *Sorry, Granny and Shelly*, he thought. *I'll give your love to Dad and Gramps.*

Klein was usually a positive guy, but despair consumed him. He wanted to protect Alivia, and he'd failed.

He followed her pointed finger and felt instant guilt for his lack of faith. A cabin. A small, pitched tin roof was less than a hundred feet in front of them. There was hope.

They upped their pace as much as they could. Alivia was half running, but it was obvious her ankle was about to give out with each step. He couldn't imagine how bad it was hurting her. He supported her the best he could, and they grew closer and closer to that cabin. Would someone be there who could help them? If not, would they even be able to get in the door? It wouldn't help to break a window and give their pursuers easy access.

He couldn't doubt the prompting that had urged him this direction, so he shelved his negative thoughts and pushed on.

They burst into the clearing surrounding the cabin. It was a small structure with two windows and a door in the front. It looked dark and quiet.

They hurried to the door and Alivia pushed on the handle. Klein shoved at the door. It screeched open and his heart leaped. They could get in. Maybe they could hunker down and defend themselves in here.

A shout came from behind them. Klein didn't look to see how close the men were. He shoved the door all the way open. Alivia hobbled in and he was close behind. He slammed the heavy wood door closed as bullets thumped into it. He was afraid they'd keep shooting, but they stopped.

Catching a breath, Klein glanced around. There was a fireplace, an old couch, a kitchen table and chairs, and some cabinets. A back door was opposite of where they stood.

It was definitely a rustic hunting cabin. A couple rifles were mounted above the fireplace. Were they just decoration? Did they have bullets in them?

Turning, he focused on the door. Alivia was right there, sliding an old-school wooden bar over the door. He was surprised and grateful it was there. They must've been prepared to keep bears out.

"Windows," she mouthed.

He nodded. The windows would be the spot they could get through.

He slid the backpack off and pulled out the gun and box of bullets. He figured she was a better shot than him, so he handed them over.

She met his gaze and something passed between them. He was acknowledging she could protect them better than he could with the gun. It was a hit to his manhood. He wanted to be the tough stud who could defend his beautiful girlfriend, but this wasn't the moment to be prideful. He yanked out both knives, handed her one, and put the other one in his pocket.

She hobbled toward the window by the kitchen table. He ran for the rifles above the fireplace. Yanking them both off, he went for the cupboards, praying there were bullets somewhere nearby.

"Beautiful Alivia," Travis shouted. He sounded far too close. Was he not concerned about them shooting him? Probably not. "Come out peacefully and we won't hurt either of you. You can lead us to the weapon, and then we'll let you go."

Silence fell outside.

Klein yanked one cupboard open. Nothing but some chipped dishes. He moved to the next one. Nothing but cans of food. Where were the bullets? Desperation clawed at him as he pulled the final cupboard open. Only a layer of dust greeted him. Oh, man.

"If we have to drag you out of there," Travis continued, "I will kill Klein and shoot you in the hand. You can still hike, but it's going to hurt, and it's goodbye to your boyfriend."

Klein spun to look at Alivia. She stared at him. Would she try to give them up? He didn't trust these guys, and he didn't want Alivia back in their power. He'd stand and fight. If only he had some bullets for one of these guns. His gut churned. How could he protect her without weapons?

She had the pistol in one hand and the bullet box was open on the floor, so he assumed she'd loaded it. Her left ankle was swollen to twice its size. She leaned against the wall by the window, standing on her right foot. If she hadn't been injured, maybe they could escape out that back door if things went badly. As it was ...

They were in so much trouble.

"Check in the chamber," she told him.

Klein blinked at her. She should be terrified or crying, but she was rationally telling him to see if the guns were already loaded. What a woman. He slid back each chamber and smiled. They were loaded. An old .22 like this usually had ten rounds.

He looked at the walls. Would they protect them from a barrage of bullets? The chinking might let bullets through. He wouldn't risk Alivia getting hit by a stray bullet. He hurried to her side, set the guns down, and slid the table closer to her. It was heavy and thick and had a rectangle shape. Perfect. He hefted it up and flipped it on its end. Then he muscled it against the log wall as a second barrier of protection for her. He slid a chair over and set it behind the table and wall. It would take more than common bullets to penetrate both.

Alivia sank into the chair, clinging to the pistol. She smiled up at him and he was overwhelmed by how much he loved her. Her blue eyes were determined, not afraid. He hefted one of the old .22 rifles but propped the other one close to her so she could reach it if she ran out of bullets in the pistol.

"Do we say anything back?" he whispered.

She grinned and nodded, then raised her voice. "Travis. I wouldn't trust you to tie your own shoes without strangling yourself. You betrayed your country. What kind of loser does that? Come and get us, you weak, lame traitors!"

Klein couldn't help but smile. She might have just written their death sentence, but he loved her fire, defiance, and bravery.

Silence met her words, but only for an instant.

Then the world exploded.

Klein ducked behind the table, crouched next to Alivia's chair, and wrapped his arms around her. Bullets thwacked loudly into the log exterior walls and the door. Both of the windows shattered and glass sprayed into the cabin, hitting Klein's back, neck, and head. It stung, but he held his position covering Alivia with his body.

As soon as the windows were gone, the men concentrated their bullets through the openings and the couch, chairs, fireplace, cupboards, and rear walls took a beating. Klein had only seen a sidearm strapped to each of the men's hips and he'd taken both large backpacks from them. The backpack Travis had carried must've been filled with some serious guns and ammo.

Seconds seemed to stretch into hours and Klein could only pray they didn't ease closer to the windows and start taking direct shots at them. How in the world would he protect Alivia?

They must've finally run out of bullets or at least needed new clips because the hailstorm slowed and then ceased. Klein released Alivia and they exchanged a look. She nodded, gripped the pistol, and stood. Holding on to the table leg, she edged to the side of the table and the shattered window.

He wanted to shelter and protect her, but he had to cover that other window. He grabbed the rifle and hurried over there. Sidling close, he looked out the window and could see Flynn grabbing a fresh clip from Travis's backpack and putting it into an A.R.

"Somebody has superior firepower," Travis called. "You ready to negotiate now?"

Alivia took aim and fired. Travis yelped in pain, so the shot must've connected. Klein smiled at that, took aim at Flynn, and fired. It hit the tree trunk next to Flynn and sprayed him with bark. Flynn cursed and scurried behind another tree.

Emboldened, Klein edged further out, cocked the gun, and

aimed at Colby. He shot and hit him in the leg. Nice. Colby cursed as his leg crumpled. He crawled behind some thick undergrowth.

"Yes!" Alivia cheered as she continued to fire at Travis.

Travis had backed away behind a tree and started returning fire. This must've emboldened the other two, as they all started unloading clips into the cabin again. Klein fired back but didn't think he hit any of his targets or even got close. He didn't dare lean out the window to have a better view.

Travis was right about one thing. The three of them definitely had superior firepower. A bullet whizzed through a gap their many shots had made in the old chinking between the logs and barely missed Klein's right ear. Too close. Klein wanted to retreat, but he couldn't. He pulled the trigger but only heard a click. Crap. He was out of ammo.

He scurried back to the table and Alivia. She was still firing with her pistol. How many bullets did she have in the magazine? The box was about half full on the floor, but he worried about her having time to reload. If he stole the other rifle, he might leave her defenseless.

Alivia looked up at him. Her blue eyes were usually so full of confidence. Right now, she looked as uncertain as he'd ever seen her. "Should we try to escape out the back door and pray they think we're still in here?" she whispered.

It wasn't a bad idea. If she could run. But what else could they do? They couldn't hold them off and this cabin would fall apart around them. Maybe somebody had heard the shots—even better, somebody who was looking for them. Maybe they could hide in the forest and pick off targets with the pistol.

"Load the pistol and put the extra bullets in your pockets," he said. "I'll carry you."

She looked like she wanted to argue, but her ankle must've hurt worse than she wanted to admit. She nodded.

More gunshots sounded out front. Klein picked up the rifle. He'd empty it out the window while she loaded the gun. Then it was time to run and pray the angels above had some miracles in store for them.

The chance to carry Alivia in his arms gave him renewed energy. That shouldn't have been so exciting, but he'd take whatever he could get.

He fired blindly out the front window, not daring to look and get a bullet between the eyes. Someone cried out in pain, and though guns were being fired, there were no bullets pounding into the cabin anymore. That didn't make sense. It was so loud and chaotic out front, and he wasn't certain about anything but their need to escape. His mind was foggy from lack of sleep and food and all the danger and uncertainty.

He heard the hammer click as he tried to fire. Empty. Turning to Alivia, he said, "Ready?"

She nodded, clinging to the pistol.

He swept her up into his arms, cradling her against his chest. She wrapped her free arm around his neck and leaned into him. Power surged through his body. He would protect the woman he loved even if it cost him his life.

Turning, he set his jaw and prayed no bullets would hit them as they crossed the small room. They'd found this cabin with heavenly direction. Somehow, they could find another spot to hide until help came. He prayed desperately for help and protection.

The back door of the cabin flung open and Travis stood there, an angry glower on his face, his dark eyes wild, and a pistol in his hand. "Time to die," he snarled.

Klein slid Alivia to her feet and stepped in front of her. He would take any bullets for her and pray she could shoot Travis before the man killed her as well.

CHAPTER ELEVEN

Cold fear raced through Alivia, a direct contrast to the heat she'd felt in Klein's arms a moment before. Travis looked unstable and furious. He aimed his pistol at Klein's chest. Klein shouldn't have stepped in front of her. She lifted her pistol and leaned around him to get a shot but feared she would be too late. Would Travis kill Klein before she could protect him?

A gun discharged, and she fired an instant too late.

"No!" she screamed, certain Klein's body would slam back into her or crumple to the ground. Please not Klein!

Travis jerked, blood spraying from his head. His body slammed to the floor as her shot hit the wall next to him.

What? Had Flynn or Colby hit him with friendly fire, or were they sick of him ordering them around? If they could kill their leader in cold blood, what would they do to her and Klein?

Klein pivoted in front of her to face whoever had shot Travis through the window.

"You all right?" Greer leaned in, an A.R. in his hands and a grim look on his face.

Alivia's legs gave out and her ankle was no support. She crumpled to the ground, releasing the pistol to the dirty wood floor.

Greer climbed through the window, but Klein pivoted and scooped her off the floor and against his chest before her cousin could reach her.

"Ali?" Klein questioned.

She cuddled into him. "I'm okay." She was so far from okay, but she had no idea what to say to reassure him.

They'd survived.

"I've got you," he whispered against her cheek, tenderly kissing her forehead.

Alivia's heart melted. Klein. He had her. He seemed to love her like she loved him.

And they had survived. The shock of that rolled over her, and she looked to where Greer had gone across the cabin to check for a pulse on Travis. He stood and shook his head. Alivia was pretty certain that was the first man Greer had ever had to kill. From the almost shocked expression in his blue eyes, she worried how he was dealing with that.

"You saved our lives," she said. "He would've killed us for sure if you hadn't shot him. Thank you."

Greer's gaze settled a bit. He was so serious she worried how he would emotionally deal with killing someone. He wouldn't talk to anybody about it, that was for sure.

"Glad you're okay," he said, three more words than the 'hey,' 'sure,' and 'yep' she usually got out of him.

"Thank you," Klein said. "How'd you know to come?"

Instead of answering, Greer walked past them, slid the bar off the door, and swung it wide.

Klein easily carried Alivia through. She clung to him with both hands around his neck. The adrenaline had already subsided, and she realized how badly her ankle throbbed. She couldn't believe how swollen it already was. They cleared the doorway, and she saw her dad and Colt out in the yard. Tears sprung to her eyes.

"Daddy," she managed. A term she hadn't called him in years.

"Livvy!" He hurried to them, his eyes widening in surprise as he saw her clinging to Klein. "I can take her."

Alivia adored her dad. She wouldn't mind a hug from him, but right now she didn't want to be out of Klein's arms.

"If it's all right with you, sir," Klein said quietly, "I'd really like to carry her."

Her dad's blue gaze flitted between them, and then he gave her a ghost of a smile. "All right. Let's get you both out of here."

He turned and Klein followed him. Alivia looked down at Flynn's motionless body and then to Colt kneeling on Colby's back. The man's face was squished into the ground, but his one dark eye was focused on her. "I'll be coming for you, beautiful," he snarled.

Colt clamped a hand over his mouth and dug his knee deeper into the man's shoulder blades. "Not the time to be making stupid threats," he growled.

"I love you, big bro," she said to Colt.

He looked at her in surprise. She wasn't the gushing type. That was Jessie. "I love you too, Livvy." His eyes seemed full of emotion. "So glad we found you."

"We prayed you here." Alivia looked up at Klein. Their gazes got all tangled up. The Lord had protected them and sent earthly help. She loved her family. She loved Klein.

Was this really going to happen? Her and Klein?

With her dad allowing this strong, amazing man to carry her to her dad's Polaris Razor side by side, she thought they had his approval. She knew they had heavenly approval, or they wouldn't be alive. Klein definitely had her approval. Did she have his?

"You and Greer good to stay until Sheriff Reed gets here to

clean up this mess?" her dad asked Colt. "I dropped him a pin with our location."

"For sure," Colt said. "Do you have some rope?"

"Yep." Her dad pulled a coil of rope out of the back of the Razor and walked it back to Colt.

Klein carried her around to the passenger side of the Razor. He let her feet slide to the ground. She tried not to put any pressure on her left ankle or wince and let him know how bad it hurt. She didn't want to be out of his arms, but she wasn't a needy woman. She never had been. She needed to remember not to be needy now. Especially because Klein was probably exhausted and hurting from everything they'd been through.

"We survived," he said.

She smiled. "You were incredible, Klein."

"I don't know about that. You have more training and expertise than I do. Toughest woman I know."

She wanted to tell him she loved him and she couldn't care less about training and expertise.

"Let's get you two home," her dad said from behind her.

Alivia startled and her cheeks filled with heat. How long had he been standing there?

Klein opened her door and helped her inside, then climbed in behind her. He had to be squished in the smaller back seat, but he didn't complain. She wanted to offer to trade him, but Klein was too much of a gentleman to accept it. Her dad loaded up, and they all secured their five-point harnesses.

They motored down a seldom-used road. The trees and undergrowth had encroached, and branches scraped the doors of her dad's custom side by side. He didn't seem to care as he asked them questions and she and Klein shared everything they'd been through. Then he told them how Shelly had discovered Klein never came home two nights ago, called Thor after midnight, and the two of them had found Klein and Alivia's trucks at the job site. They had feared foul play and alerted the rest of the family and the sheriff's department. Everyone had searched for them, spreading out throughout the mountains with Greer, Colt, and her dad taking the area north and east of the ski resort. When they'd heard the guns firing, they'd rushed in their direction and found them.

The Razor finally made it to their little valley. Nothing had ever looked so good. Her mom and Aunt Myrna were waiting for them outside. They both rushed up to her door and flipped out over her ankle and how dirty she looked. They all but lifted her out of the razor, each with an arm around her, and tried to usher her into her parents' house to doctor her up, bathe, and feed her. Food and a bath sounded great, but she didn't want to leave Klein.

"Klein." She tried to turn and look at him. He stood next to the Razor looking incredibly tough and appealing with his clothes all ripped and dirty. He also looked like he didn't know what his place was or what he should be doing.

"Oh, Klein." Her mom turned back to him. "Thank you for protecting my girl." She released Alivia and Aunt Myrna tightened her grip. Her mom ran to Klein, gave him a bear hug, and said, "Thank you. I'm going to bring you the biggest gift basket you've ever seen."

Klein smiled, but it seemed strained. A gift basket? That was nice, but Alivia wanted to be all he'd ever need.

"Joseph will run you home," her mom continued. "I know Shelly and Granny have been beside themselves."

His face changed, filling with concern for his family. "Thank you." He focused on Alivia and tilted his chin up. "I'll be back soon."

"Okay."

It was lame, but it had to be enough. For now. With her mom, aunt, and dad watching on, she couldn't do what she longed to. She wanted to give Klein many, many kisses of gratitude. Talk about their future. What would she tell him about the Delta family secret? Could she tell him anything? He was involved at this point. Shelly and Bailey had been brought into the circle of trust. There was no reason Klein couldn't be.

If he was interested in being part of the family.

Her dad loaded back into the Razor, gesturing Klein inside. Klein climbed up front and within seconds they were roaring past. Klein caught her gaze one more time. It was enough. Right? Everything was a muddled mess in her mind with how tired she was, but she could remember those kisses. Did that mean he loved her like she loved him or was it just because they'd been thrust together and he'd kissed her because she was there?

No. He'd given her sweet compliments and said any man would want to date and kiss her, but most importantly that he would. He'd been willing to give his life for her. If only she wasn't so tired and could remember how he'd phrased everything and discern what it all could mean for them.

Alivia had difficulty keeping her mom and aunt from discovering how deeply she loved Klein as she let them doctor up her ankle. She escaped to take a bath, with one leg hanging out of the tub, before grabbing some food and being informed that everyone was meeting at Papa's to figure out what was going on. Would Klein come for her while she wasn't available?

The family gathered in Papa's conference room. Alivia was exhausted and couldn't think straight. They repeated the same information time and again, trying to figure out who had sent Travis, Flynn, and Colby. Hoping Colby would be more willing to talk when they could interrogate him again. Wondering if Admiral Seamons could truly be their leak. Worrying about some military leader, a Commander Frederick who claimed to be descended from Frederick the Great and thought he was the rightful leader of

Europe. The man had overthrown the government of the small country of Banida in Eastern Europe and was gaining power and support. They were afraid his next target was Poland. That was a concern not just for the world stage but for them personally, as their friend Melene had been relocated to Poland on a volunteer assignment with refugees.

The most interesting moment came when Papa asked, "Do any of you remember Admiral Seamons' granddaughter, Kylee?"

"Greer does," Thor teased as only a brother could.

Greer's tanned face darkened, but he broke his usual silence. "Not me. Chandler."

Everyone nodded and some exchanged smirks. Alivia remembered Chandler sneaking off into the trees a time or two when Kylee had stayed with them in the summer as a teenager. Greer had only dated one girl as far as she knew and Belinda had ended things between them and left the valley a couple years ago.

Papa's brows rose, but he didn't say anything. "Kylee is a highly accomplished linguist and educator. She contacted me last night, confused and upset. She claimed she intercepted communication that she believes is a request from Commander Frederick to meet with Admiral Seamons."

The room exploded with questions, ideas, worries, but not enough answers. Alivia's family was understandably upset and concerned with this tidbit, but until they could validate it, what could they do? They determined the need to hire a private investigator to keep tabs on Seamons and see what came of it. The rest of them needed to stay close to home; these events pointed to protecting the secret being more important than ever. What if Seamons had already exposed the secret to this Frederick? Was that who had paid Travis, Flynn, and Colby to come after them?

Alivia struggled to keep her eyes open and focus on the conversation. Where was Klein? When would she see him again? She laid her head on her arms and listened. Kind of.

Suddenly, strong arms were carrying her.

"Klein," she murmured, leaning into him.

"Gross, sis," Colt's voice came. "Don't think I'm loverboy and try to kiss me or something."

Alivia struggled to come fully awake, but she was too tired.

"Mom's making me carry you to their house so you can sleep. I want to rewrap your ankle. Don't tell Mom or Aunt Myrna."

"But Klein," she tried to argue.

"You can see him tomorrow."

A soft pillow and mattress met her a minute later. She stayed awake while Colt checked and rewrapped her ankle but just barely. She fought the exhaustion, but it was too strong. She wanted to get a message to Klein, but darkness pulled her under before she could act on the desire.

CHAPTER TWELVE

Alivia's dad dropped Klein off at home about seven-thirty that morning. He ate while Shelly grilled him, but when he tried to turn the tables on her and ask about the Deltas' secret, she clammed up. She got a text and took off, claiming she had to go meet with the Deltas. He was jealous and had so many questions. What was the weapon or secret the men had been after? Alivia's dad, brother, and cousin had showed up like some special forces team and easily taken down three trained soldiers. Who did that? Alivia was obviously an expert fighter as well.

He wanted to know Alivia's every secret, and he wanted to be part of the Delta family. Was that going to happen for him? Was Alivia going to be in his life? It felt like it. He could hope and pray.

Wendy, the morning nurse, showed up at eleven. Klein should've gone and checked on job sites, or driven straight back to Alivia, but he didn't know if he'd be welcomed into some Delta family meeting. He took a shower and then lay down on his bed, setting an alarm so he wouldn't sleep all day.

The alarm startled him at two. He woke, dressed more carefully than he normally did, brushed his teeth, and put on his favorite PBR Black & Blue Cologne. He kissed Granny goodbye and took Wendy's teasing as he left. Thankfully, somebody had brought his truck back. The sheriff needed to question him, according to his voicemail. He'd respond soon. Right now, he needed to see Alivia. He loaded up and drove far too fast to Alivia's house. There were trucks, dirt bikes, and side by sides parked in Papa's driveway, but Alivia's house was quiet and she didn't respond to him ringing the doorbell.

He didn't know how to take on the entire Delta crew, and he'd reveal his hand completely if any of them saw his face when he asked for Alivia. He left a note on her door, telling her he'd been there and to please call him on their home phone or Shelly's phone. Who knew what Travis had done with their cell phones?

He walked back to his truck and almost wimped out and drove out of the valley, but he needed her too much. They'd gone through something insane together and it was the change he'd been hoping for. They'd kissed and he'd told her how incredible she was. Now it was time to see how to meld their lives together.

Stopping in front of Papa's house, he climbed out of his truck and was met by Colt. "Hey, man." Colt slapped him on the shoulder. "I just carried Livvy up to Papa's guest room to get some rest, but she thought I was you." He winked.

Klein's heart thumped faster. "That's ... good." It had to be good. Right? "Should I ... let her sleep?"

"Probably. Sorry, but she was tuckered out."

"Okay. I'll come by later. Thanks for coming for us earlier."

"For sure." Colt waved to him and headed across the gravel toward his house.

Klein looked around. He wanted to sit by Alivia while she slept, but that would push boundaries for sure.

He slowly climbed back into his truck and drove into town to meet with the sheriff and answer his questions. After that, he did a round of checking on the closer job sites and used one of the worker's phones to check on the other projects. All the workers had a lot of questions about what had happened to him and Alivia. Klein had absolutely no idea how to answer. He skirted the questions, checked on things, and was back home by six-thirty, wondering how soon he could go find Alivia again.

Kelsey and Mo were there with Granny. Shoot. Of course; they would be there until seven. He walked into the house and everybody's faces lit up.

"Klein." Granny clapped her hands together happily. "Will you marry Kelsey so Mo can have a daddy?"

Kelsey's shocked expression matched his own. At least she hadn't put Granny up to the question. As they stared at each other, Kelsey's face morphed into a hopeful look and a sweet, welcoming smile that made his gut churn with apprehension. What could he say that wouldn't hurt this young mom? Kelsey was great, but she wasn't Alivia.

"Um ..." Could he claim he and Alivia were dating? Not really. And if it all backfired, Alivia would not appreciate him spouting off about them being together. But they were together. Right?

"Klein!" Mo rushed up to him and tugged at his legs. "Let's go play outside!"

Klein happily swooped the little boy into his arms. "We'll go play out back."

Granny smiled as if nothing was amiss. Kelsey seemed to give him a longing look. He needed to set her straight, but he couldn't do that with Granny looking on and hoping he'd marry the girl. Yikes.

He hurried out through the garage, grabbing a football on the way. He and Mo went around to the backyard and the stretch of grass that butted against the mountains. They played catch for a while and then a game of sorts started where he'd toss Mo the football and Mo would catch it, or scoop it off the ground if he missed, and then take off running. Klein would chase him and softly tackle him to the grass. They'd roll around for a minute laughing before doing it all over again.

A truck roared up to the house, but he wasn't sure if it was Shelly or Thor. Wait—it had to be Shelly. Thor's truck was a quiet, new diesel. Shelly was here. That would help. Kelsey would come for Mo, and he could nicely explain that he was dating someone else. Hopefully she wouldn't pin him down to who.

The back door to the garage opened, and he heard footsteps. He looked over and sure enough, Kelsey was coming across the lawn toward them. She smiled brightly at him. He waved.

"Klein, you gotta chase me," Mo hollered.

Klein laughed. He took off after Mo and chased him around. He tackled him close to where Kelsey was standing. She laughed at their silly game. They rolled around and somehow they knocked into Kelsey's legs and Mo grabbed his mom's ankle, yanking her right on top of the two of them.

"Sorry," Klein managed, trying to scramble away, but he was tangled up with Mo in his arms and Kelsey somehow wrapped around him from the side with her face right close to his.

"I don't mind," she said sweetly. "Thank you for playing with him."

"I love playing with Mo." How could he get away without rudely pushing her off of him? "I need to go check on Granny. Let me walk you to your car. Is Shelly here?" He rushed all of this out almost as one sentence.

"I think so. At least I heard a truck when I was heading out here." She was staring at his lips. This was bad.

Klein slid out from under her and stood with Mo in his arms. Mo clung to his neck, prattling about how fast he was. Kelsey was still oddly lying on the grass, blinking up at Klein with long-lashed, dark eyes. He offered her a hand up. She took it and as he pulled, she pressed into his chest, wrapping her arms around his back. This was not going well.

"Klein," she said softly, licking her lips. He was sure for many other men this sweet, beautiful, smart mom would be impossible to resist, but not for him.

He stepped back. "I'm dating someone seriously," he blurted out. So much for letting her down easy.

"Oh." She also stepped back and reached out a hand to Mo.

"I'm sorry," he managed, setting Mo on the ground.

A door slammed out front and a truck motor started.

"It's fine," she said. "I'm sorry. I just made this awkward."

"Not your fault." He heard the truck racing away. What was going on with Shelly?

"This won't mess up my job, will it?" she asked quietly.

"Oh, no. Not at all. Granny loves you and Mo. Shelly and I are so grateful for you taking good care of her."

"Okay. Thanks." She blinked up at him. She was a beautiful woman, but she wasn't Alivia. She took Mo's hand and tried to hurry her boy away, obviously embarrassed by the entire interaction and conversation.

"Bye, Klein," Mo hollered. "Thanks for playing!"

Klein smiled and waved. "Any time." He had the strangest feeling as he looked into Mo's eyes. Those were Delta eyes. Eyes like Alivia's. Was he seeing Alivia everywhere, or was there a possibility one of the Delta boys...?

No way. They were all too respectful of women and too good of Christians to get a young girl pregnant and then desert her to raise their son on her own. The two of them disappeared around the garage.

He waited for a beat, then hurried in to check on Granny. They made dinner together and he tried to explain that he wasn't going to marry Kelsey, but she didn't seem to be listening. Where was Shelly?

They'd eaten and cleaned up before Shelly came rushing in. "Sorry. I was with the Deltas earlier, then stayed at work a little late."

He nodded. "I want to go check on Alivia again."

She grinned hugely. "Go, then. I won't wait up." Her smile faltered. "Actually, can you please let me know when you come home? It was terrifying not knowing where you were and thinking you were kissing on Alivia but finding out the two of you had been kidnapped."

"Kissing Alivia?" Granny's brow wrinkled in confusion. "Kidnapped?"

He probably should stay and help with Granny.

"I've got this." Shelly waved him off, then blew him a kiss. "Go find her, bro."

Klein gave Shelly and Granny each a hug and then rushed out of the house and to his truck. Once again, he drove like a madman up to the Deltas' valley. He was probably going to get a ticket. He could talk Reed out of one, but probably not one of his deputies.

The beautiful valley looked a lot quieter now. The sun was close to setting and there weren't dirt bikes, side by sides, and trucks piled at Papa's. Everybody was probably at their own houses.

Alivia. At her own house. Would she be alone? He hoped so.

He drove straight there and hurried to the door. He tilted his head to the side, surprised that his note was still attached.

He rang the doorbell. Nothing. He pounded for a bit. Nothing. Worry pulsed through him. Was she okay? What should he do? He couldn't even text or call her. Pushing down the latch, he quietly let himself inside. "Ali?" he called.

Nothing.

Where was she? He needed her more than he needed water or air or food or ... he was being silly, but he needed her badly. How did he keep missing her?

He walked back out onto the porch. Which house should he try first? Neither he nor Alivia had cell phones. Travis had probably destroyed them so they couldn't be traced. Dang. He rapped his fist against his thigh and trudged to his truck.

"Hey, Klein." Thor walked past, heading to his house.

"Hey, have you seen Alivia?"

Thor studied him, and those blue eyes made Klein want to find Alivia even more. "She's staying at her mom and dad's tonight. Apparently she's pretty shaken up from ... everything that happened."

That made sense. Klein could understand that. She'd been incredibly brave and tough, but she was probably a mess. "You think they'll care if I ... check on her?"

Thor studied him. "You like my cousin, huh?"

He nodded. What could he say? Thor and Shelly were engaged and all head over heels in love. If anybody could understand, it would be Thor. Klein felt excitement and joy race through him. Was it finally his and Alivia's turn?

"Good luck, man. Livvy's awesome but not great at the emotional junk, you know?"

"I know," Klein admitted. "But neither was Shelly."

Thor chuckled at that. "She's an expert at it now. Especially the kissing."

"Okay, that'll do." Klein held up a hand to ward off his future brother-in-law saying any more.

Thor laughed and walked off. "See you soon."

"Yep." Klein hurried to his truck and drove down the short stretch to Alivia's mom's house. He could've run it, but he was pretty wiped out from their crazy adventure. If he could call if that.

Though if the experience had brought Alivia into his life and arms, he'd call it whatever she wanted.

He hurried to her parents' front porch and rang the doorbell. Her dad opened it and his face softened when he saw Klein. "Hey. How are you holding up?"

He didn't invite him inside. Dang.

"Great. Thanks. I got a nap, a shower, and some food. Alivia?" He tried to look over her dad's shoulder.

"She's lying down." Her dad stepped onto the porch and shut the door behind him. Dang. This was not going well. "I've never seen her cry like that."

Klein started forward. He had to go to her. Hold her. Was she having a post-traumatic emotional hit of what they'd gone through? She'd dealt with everything so well. She always had to be so tough. He admired and loved that about her, but he wanted to be there for her when she was struggling. "Can I ..."

"I think you'd better let her sleep this off." Her dad's voice wasn't mean, but he wouldn't let Klein in there to hold his daughter in their guest bedroom. Dang. "I'll tell her you stopped by. Neither of you have a phone?"

"No, sir." Stopped by? That wasn't good enough.

"Okay. I'll have her call Shelly or call your house." Alivia's father patted him on the shoulder. "Thanks again for watching out for her."

"Of course." Klein needed to tell this man that he loved his daughter. No, he couldn't tell her dad before he told her. But he had to send some kind of message to Alivia.

"Oh, and Klein." Joseph's jaw worked. "I hope you understand not to say anything about the ... secret those men were after."

Klein's brows went up. Nobody had even broached this subject with him. Even Reed had been cryptic in his answers. He looked over her dad. He'd always thought all the Deltas looked like military machines. Could her dad take him down if Klein said no? He wasn't about to mess up a future with Alivia over some secret or weapon or whatever it was, no matter how curious he was about it. It was disconcerting to go his whole life thinking he knew this family and lived in a safe, boring valley and then to have that flipped on its head. The fact that it was Alivia's family protecting this secret or weapon made him even more curious.

"Oh, no sir." He didn't even dare ask questions. Maybe after he married Alivia? He also didn't dare go to marriage, even in his mind. It was too early and exciting to let his brain wander that direction.

"Thank you, Klein. I think Papa will brief you later, but ... we're trying to keep a wrap on this thing. I'm afraid it's going to explode on us." He gave a grim smile. "It'll all work out. Right?"

"Sure." Klein didn't know. He had no idea about anything. All that really mattered to him was working things out with Alivia. Then he could figure out her big family secret and whether they wanted him to help, as Shelly was doing.

"Good man." Joseph patted his shoulder again, then went in and shut the door.

Klein stood there for a moment longer. What had just happened? Was it over? He'd somehow lost any opportunity to talk to Alivia tonight. He stood there for probably too long, but he understood her dad was telling him to give her some space. She was upset. He'd never seen her cry so hard? Dang. If only Klein could hold and comfort her like he wanted to.

He stared at the door, willing it to open.

Nothing.

No open door. No Alivia in his arms. This stunk.

After far too long, he gave up and trudged to his truck. Tomorrow, he'd find her. He'd figure it all out. Then he could hold her, kiss her, tell her he loved her, list all the things he loved about her. What kind of ring would Alivia want? Not some flashy diamond.

He'd seen cool wedding bands that were studded with smaller diamonds and flush with the band so they wouldn't catch on anything. He'd research a ring like that tonight, after he worked for a few hours. Working himself into exhaustion and then looking for rings was nothing close to holding and kissing Alivia, but at least it would give him something to occupy his brain.

CHAPTER THIRTEEN

Alivia woke from her nap that had begun during the meeting. It was six-ten in the evening, and she was in Papa's guest bedroom. The family had dispersed, but her mom was only too happy to tell her that Klein had been by to see her. Colt had been the one to speak with him. It took some doing, but she finally shuffled away from her concerned family and headed for Klein's house. She drove way too fast. She could hardly wait to see him.

She pulled up front and shut the truck off. An old, rusted Honda sat in the driveway next to Klein's truck. Kelsey's car? Her gut churned, but that was silly. Kelsey was Granny's nurse, and she worked until seven. It was only six-forty-five. Nothing to worry about.

Klein had kissed Alivia, complimented her, protected her, and told her he wanted to date her. She was no relationship expert, but she was pretty sure that meant the man of her dreams loved her. Their time together was a bit foggy, but she remembered his sweet words and his kisses and how he'd protected her and how incredible he was.

She slowly made it to the front door and knocked. Granny pulled the door open and smiled at her, but it was kind of blank. Did Granny not remember her? She knew Granny was having more and more memory loss, but she usually remembered Alivia.

"Hi, Granny," she managed, balancing on mostly her right leg. It seemed rude to tell Granny who she was. "Is Klein here?"

"Oh, yes." Granny beamed, grabbed her hand, and tugged her forward. It hurt to put more pressure on her left ankle, but she didn't care. She would see Klein.

Alivia's heart raced. Klein was here and Granny was happily leading Alivia to him. Yay. All of her girlish dreams were about to come true.

She and Granny walked hand in hand through the entryway and into the living room. She loved how Klein had fixed up this entire house. It was beautiful. He was beautiful. Manly and beautiful.

She didn't see Klein anywhere, but Granny kept walking until they reached the picture windows overlooking the backyard.

"There he is." Granny pointed.

Alivia could only stare. Shock and then horror raced through her. She leaned into the window frame for support. Klein was lying on the grass. With Mo and Kelsey both on top of him. What?

She tried to back away, but Granny still held her hand.

Granny looked at her. "See? My Klein is marrying Kelsey. Won't he make the best dad for Mo?"

Alivia stuttered, but nothing came out. She looked back out the window as Klein climbed to his feet with Mo in his arms. His back was to her, but he reached out a hand and lifted the gorgeous, petite, feminine Kelsey to her feet. Kelsey cuddled in close to him, wrapping her arms around his strong back. It was perfect. They were perfect.

Alivia was nauseated.

"Excuse me," she managed, then she pulled her hand from Granny's grip and shuffle-stepped quickly from the house.

She made it to her truck and somehow drove back home. Tears ran down her face; she could hardly see through them. She angled for her house, but as she drove past her parents, her dad was out there, flagging her down.

She didn't want to talk to anybody, see anybody. She needed to go home and cry her eyes out. Klein and Kelsey? It made so much sense. Had they really told Granny they were getting married? How could he have kissed Alivia like that early this morning? She wanted to be furious with him, but she hurt too much. The anger would come later.

She stopped the truck and put it in gear. Her dad was right there. He pulled the door open, took one look at her, and murmured, "Oh, Livvy, what happened?"

Shaking her head, she tried to say, "I'm fine," but who knew what blubbering nonsense came out.

"Come on, my girl. I've got you now." Her dad easily lifted her out of the truck as if she were still a child. He'd kept himself ultra-fit just like Papa and Uncle Keith had. They left her truck there in the road. Running. Somebody would come along and take care of it.

She let him carry her into the house. Her mom started asking a million questions, but he simply held up his hand and she followed them up the stairs to the guest suite. Her mom pulled back the covers and her dad laid her down. Then her mom took off her shoes and they both tucked the covers over her.

She squinted up at them. It was impossible to see through her bleary eyes.

"Ah, my girl. I can't imagine how scared you were, how traumatic it all was ... but I'm so glad Klein was there. Those men didn't ... take advantage of you?"

She shook her head and managed, "No." Her dad looked reassured, but she still felt awful. Klein. He'd been there for her. The tears came harder. Oh, Klein. Now he would be there for Kelsey and Mo.

She rolled onto her side and curled into a ball. Would this pain ever stop? Of course it would. She was tough, and she had her family. She'd never dared believe she and Klein would be together forever. That's why she'd avoided revealing her feelings for him for so long.

Somehow, last night she'd let herself believe they would work. Dang it, that had been dumb. She'd let herself fall so hard for him. Actually, that wasn't true. She'd already fallen for him. She'd let herself believe her dreams were coming true and said things she shouldn't have and kissed him. Oh man, had she kissed him.

Her mom fussed about how she was supposed to meet with the sheriff. Her dad said it could wait. Her parents kneeled by her bedside and they each took one of her hands. Her dad said a lengthy prayer of gratitude for their safety and protection. A prayer of healing and strength and her ability to feel her family's love and the deep love from her Savior. She appreciated it. She felt their faith and love wash over her.

The prayer finished and her dad stood and walked to a large easy chair close by and settled down as if he'd watch over her. Her mom sat next to her on the bed, gently massaged her scalp, and sang song after song about Jesus.

Alivia must've fallen asleep. She woke to a dark house. Her mom was sleeping next to her, and her dad was asleep in the chair. He looked uncomfortable. She loved them so much. Some of the pain was less, but then the picture of Klein and Kelsey hit her again and it all came back.

No. She would not cry.

The alarm clock read four-fifty a.m. She had to have fallen asleep before eight last night. Far too much sleep.

She slipped quietly out of bed and used the bathroom, then padded downstairs and found a pad of paper and a pen. Her ankle was tender but felt much better than yesterday. The way Colt had re-wrapped it had taken the swelling down and supported it pretty well. She wrote her parents a quick note telling them how much she loved them and how grateful she was. She promised she was fine, and that she was heading to work. She'd talk to Sheriff Reed after.

Then she hobbled to her house, slipping in through the garage entrance. Someone had returned her truck—good. Work would be a nightmare without a phone, but everything felt like a nightmare without Klein, so she'd deal with one thing at a time.

She went to her home office and checked the messages. There were a lot. She got online and figured out how to order a phone with her same phone number. Luckily, her phone messages were attached to her computer, so she answered all the messages and emails she could deal with. Thankfully, Klein had gone in yesterday and dealt with some fires. He was a great work partner. Sadly, that was all he could be.

She sniffled, wiped away the stupid tears, and got back to work.

It was before five-thirty when she showered, put on some work clothes, grabbed a protein shake and a water bottle, and headed for the job site with the most fires. It was, unfortunately, the Nelson home. The spot she and Klein had been kidnapped. The spot they'd almost connected. The spot they'd done finish work together. Would Klein show up here? Oh, how she hoped not. She wasn't ready to pretend she was all right or deal with him dating Kelsey.

Nobody was there when she arrived, so she started puttying some of the cherry wood baseboards. The finish work guys showed up at six. They usually started at seven, but they were as worried as she was about getting this job done. They all hoped Klein would show up soon.

She didn't.

She claimed she was fine, that the kidnapping was a big mistake and no big deal, and asked how she could help them get this job done. They didn't ask too many questions and put her to work. Thank heavens.

It was good to focus on work. She'd work herself into oblivion. It was her only hope to keep her sanity and keep her distance from Klein. How could she work with him after kissing him like that and knowing he was with Kelsey? Her stomach dropped as she imagined the gorgeous wedding those two would have. Mo would be so adorable walking down the aisle with his radiantly beautiful mother. Klein would be so handsome waiting for the two of them in a dark gray tux and orange tie, his green eyes lit up.

Alivia had to pause and put a hand to her stomach. She was going to puke.

"Boss?" Jayden was next to her, puttying. "You all right?"

"Sure." She would never be all right again, but it wasn't this guy's problem.

The front door flung open and loud footsteps stormed through the entryway. Alivia stood, balancing mostly on her right foot, and clung to the putty and rag in her hand.

Klein cleared the arched entryway and his green eyes focused right on her. "Ali ..." His voice was so full of longing she had to lean against the wall for support. All she wanted to do was run to him.

He crossed the space and their men kept working around them, though she was sure they were sneaking glances. All she could see was Klein's handsome face.

He reached her and looked her over. "Are you all right?"

"Fine." She tilted her chin. "We've got a deadline. I think they could use you in the master finishing up the crown moldings."

She tried to turn, but he gently caught her arm and turned her to face him. He wrapped his hands around the backs of her arms.

"Ali. I've been going insane worrying about you. I went by your house and Colt said you were taking a nap. Did you get my note?"

Note? She shook her head no.

"Then I came back later that evening and you were asleep at your parents' house. Your dad said he'd never seen you cry so hard. I wanted to hold you, but I didn't know how to push your dad out of the way." He gave her half a smile. "I'm sorry that you were so upset."

Her eyes widened. He should be sorry. Was he sorry he was marrying Kelsey or just sorry she was upset? He needed to stop touching her so she could summon a rational response. He was making this even harder than it had to be.

"We can talk about this later," she forced out. "Not while we're at a job site."

His brow furrowed. "This can't wait."

Oh, it could wait. She'd avoid talking to him as long as she possibly could. "Not around the guys," she said through gritted teeth.

His eyes filled with understanding. "Gotcha." He released her arms, and she thought he might listen and let her work. All she wanted was to work.

Okay, she was a pathetic liar. All she wanted was him.

He focused on her face and warmth filled her. No! She couldn't keep thinking there was something romantic between them. Work. That was it. She tried to back away but hit the wall.

Klein's gaze filled with determination. He took the rag and putty from her hands and dropped them.

"What are you doing?" she asked.

He didn't answer. He bent down and slid one arm under her thighs and one under her back, then swooped her off the ground.

"What are you doing?" she demanded again, but it came out far too breathy. She wanted to wrap her arms around his broad back, lay her head in the crook of his neck, and just hold on to him forever.

"You said not around the guys. I'm carrying you outside so we can talk. How's your ankle?"

"I don't want to talk to you," she protested.

"Sorry, love. I've been going insane. I hardly slept. I couldn't find you yesterday or this morning. We are going to talk this out."

He walked through the main room. She loved how decisive and tough he was. He was such an incredible man. But he could never be her incredible man.

Sorry, love? He wanted to talk this out? Oh, she'd give him a talk.

"Go marry Kelsey," she yelled. "And leave me alone."

"Kelsey?" His footsteps faltered and he stared at her, his face far too close. "Why would I marry Kelsey?"

She folded her arms across her chest and glowered at him. "Granny told me you were marrying her."

Klein shook his head. He carried her through the entryway, out the still open front door, and onto the porch.

He lowered her to her feet but kept his arms around her, supporting her and holding her far too close for comfort. "Ali ... Granny has dementia. You realize that, right?"

"She seemed very lucid to me," she insisted, jutting out her chin. "And I saw you in your backyard, holding Kelsey and Mo. You looked like the perfect little family."

His eyes filled with comprehension. "You were the truck that came and then left. I thought it was Shelly."

"It was me," she admitted, stepping back and leaning against the side of the house for support. She was weak all over, and her ankle suddenly throbbed.

Klein's arms dropped from around her. "Ali. Mo and I were playing in the yard. We rolled too close to Kelsey and she fell on top of us. When I could get away from her, I offered her a hand up and she wrapped her arms around me. I promise you. I'm not marrying her, and I didn't hold her."

Alivia stared at him. She bit at her cheek and said in a small voice, "You looked perfect together. Mo is so adorable and Kelsey is so beautiful and feminine—"

Klein stepped close and pinned her against the house. "Ali ... nobody is perfect for me but you. No other woman is as beautiful as you. Not to me, at least."

Alivia could hardly believe this. She'd been so certain he wanted Kelsey and he'd just inadvertently let down his guard with Alivia in the mountains. But she knew how loyal and good Klein was. It hit her hard. He wouldn't have kissed her if he loved Kelsey.

Klein framed her face with his hands and leaned in close. "I love you, Ali. Only you. I've loved you for so long, but I had no clue how to break the barrier of employee or partner or whatever. The kidnapping was awful, and I was terrified you'd get hurt, but if it brought us together, it was worth it."

She stared into his green eyes and grasped his biceps for stability. "You love me?" she squeaked.

"I do. You're everything to me, Ali." He searched her face. "The question is, do you feel the same?"

She nodded and admitted roughly, "I do."

Klein softly kissed her and the world finally righted itself. He whispered against her mouth, "Will you say it, love?"

She managed a smile, though she was trembling. "I love you, Klein Vance, you suave, sexy stud," she stole Jessie's description of him. "I love you and only you."

"Yes!" he yelled, and then he pressed her into the house and devoured her mouth with his.

Cheering sounded from inside the house and Alivia realized they hadn't closed the front door. The guys were probably watching their bosses make out through the huge windows.

She didn't care.

She returned the pressure of Klein's kiss, slid her arms around his neck, and lifted herself closer to him. She loved this man. Nothing else mattered at this moment except him. Their future might be busy and maybe rocky protecting the Delta secret and taking care of Granny, but they'd make it work. Together.

Thank you for reading Klein and Alivia's story! I love them together. Greer and Emery's story is next. It's intense and romantic and I honestly didn't know how they were going to overcome the huge obstacles between them. So fun! Keep reading for an excerpt.

Hugs and thanks,

Cami

Delta Family Romances

Deceived

Abandoned

Committed

Betrayed

Devoted

Compromised

Endangered

BETRAYED - EXCERPT

Greer Delta finished feeding and watering his horses and then walked out of his barn into the summer evening. It was the first of July, and absolutely beautiful in his family's remote, lush mountain valley. He wandered over to the fence line where his steers were grazing. The fence line stretched up into the trees and then a mile to the south end of the valley, the lake was the eastern boundary.

He'd built his house, barn, and corrals a half a mile around the lake, distancing himself from the rest of his family. He loved his family. They were great people and they had his back. He craved privacy and needed quiet. They'd all been respectful of that.

Since he'd killed a man last week he'd had this unfamiliar urge for human company and contact. Which made no sense to him and would've confused everyone who knew him. If he'd been willing to open his mouth and talk to anybody about it.

His mom claimed even as a child he'd been sober and would arch away from anyone wanting to hold him close. Probably a character flaw. He didn't know, but he also wasn't one to waste time stewing about his silence or anybody's interpretation of it. He worked hard on his ranch, raising the best beef cattle in Colorado. He trained diligently as part of the Delta Protection Detail to protect a secret that he didn't even have the privilege of knowing. He didn't ask questions or seek out anyone's attention. With the exception of Belinda, the other women he'd kissed had initiated the dating and the kissing. He'd liked it. A lot. But he'd never found a woman besides Belinda that he craved being with enough to give up his peaceful, contented life. If he got bored he turned on a country song.

Not contented any more, and no country song could distract him from the anguish. In his dreams and during the day he could still see it. Uncle Joseph, Colt, and him had searched together for a day and a half, not sleeping and barely eating or drinking. Papa, his dad, and Thor had been searching other spots of the mountains along with Sheriff Reed and some trusted friends from town.

He, Uncle Joseph, and Colt had finally heard gunshots and found the men who'd kidnapped Klein and Alivia decimating an old cabin in the woods.

His Uncle Joseph had shot and killed one of the men out front while Greer and his cousin Colt had tackled the other one. Colt pinned the guy down and told Greer to find Alivia. With the two aggressors subdued Greer had rushed for the decimated windows of the little cabin, hoping his cousin Alivia and her business partner Klein were still alive, and wondering where Travis Reeder had disappeared to.

He'd found all three of them. The mercenary and kidnapper was framed in the back door of the cabin, pointing a gun at Klein and Alivia, and saying, "It's time to die."

Greer passed a hand over his face, no longer seeing the peaceful green meadow bordered by the lake, the thick trees, the picturesque mountain, and the blue summer sky.

His semi-automatic rifle had already been in his hand and ready to fire. He'd reacted on instinct born of years and years of training by his grandpa, an elite military man. He'd fired before Travis Reeder could kill Klein or Alivia. He'd shot Reeder straight through the head and everybody had proclaimed him a hero.

He was no hero. He'd just reacted to protect his cousin and his friend. Everyone assumed he was being humble about saving their lives, not taking credit because Greer never wanted anyone to fuss over him. The truth was, it was a horrific weight to have taken a man's life. Even if the man was a mercenary, a deserter, hired to steal the Delta secret, had resorted to kidnapping to do it, and been willing to kill for a huge paycheck.

Papa seemed to be the only one who understood Greer pulling into himself even deeper. His grandfather had spent years in the military. Greer had never asked how many men he'd had to kill, but he knew it had happened. Papa had come over twice in the past week, brought takeout and watched a couple of Chandler's lacrosse games with Greer. Chandler was a huge success in the PLL and they were all very proud.

Last night Papa had come over and showed him the footage of Travis Reeder's graveside service. It was held at a pretty cemetery in Salmon, Idaho. There had only been four people at the ten-minute long service: the preacher, an older couple Papa explained were Reeder's foster parents throughout high school, and a sister.

Emery Reeder. She'd been much, much prettier than the beautiful setting. Long dark curly hair, deep-brown eyes, and an angelic-looking face.

It had ripped him apart to see the silent tears tracing down her face as she buried her only family member.

Why Papa had felt he needed to watch the service he couldn't say, but he'd sat and watched it without saying anything. Not that Greer ever said much. Then he'd listened as Papa told him that Miss Reeder was a schoolteacher in Nevada, no criminal history, loved by her students and their parents, seemed to be an upstanding citizen. She and Travis had been shuffled through foster care, she'd put herself through Boise State University while Travis had joined the military. Who knew why Travis had gone AWOL and become a mercenary, but his sister looked to be doing good things.

And Greer was responsible for leaving her without family. Here he was surrounded by loving family, but he'd taken Emery Reeder's only brother.

Papa focused the power of his penetrating blue gaze on him and said, "I know what you're going through. I've been there. All the reassurances that you had no choice but to take that shot, that Reeder would've killed Klein or Alivia if you hadn't, aren't going to help. I have to ask one thing though. If you wouldn't have reacted instinctively and taken that shot and Alivia or Klein were dead, would you have been able to live with yourself any better?"

Greer's eyes widened. "No," he admitted. Of course he would've chosen to protect Alivia and Klein and the fact remained that Reeder had kidnapped them so he could discover the Delta family secret for a fat paycheck and had been about to kill one of them because it hadn't gone according to his plan and he was furious.

"I didn't think so." Papa took a breath and said, "You've taken a life, Greer. It's one of the hardest things to reconcile in your mind and heart because life is precious and we've been commanded not to kill. Throughout the scriptures there are many, many examples of times God's people had to kill. Killing Travis Reeder wasn't optional and I'm so grateful you didn't hesitate, that you fired instinctively and protected Alivia and Klein. But I also can't tell you what it means to me that you're not taking the responsibility lightly. The very fact that I can see the torture in your eyes tells me your heart is soft and you would never hurt someone needlessly."

Greer's heart beat painfully against his ribs. Papa understood. Of course he did.

"Will it stop hurting?" he asked.

"In time, and with prayer."

Greer needed to pray, but he'd felt too stirred up. He pointed at the computer they'd watched the graveside service on. "How do I help?"

"I don't know that you can help Emery Reeder, but you can pray for her."

Greer nodded slowly. Maybe he couldn't pray for himself yet, but he could pray for her.

"God will help her." Papa's gaze got even more intense. "And He will help you. Only your Savior can take away the pain. Turn to Him Greer. Always turn to Him."

That hit him hard. He knew Papa was right. And he wanted to move past the pain and find peace.

So he'd spent hours last night that he should've been sleeping praying for Emery Reeder and praying the good Lord could make things right for that lady and that she could find peace and comfort.

He stared at the cows munching on grass and realized the sun was setting. Dang, he was good at wasting time lately. No one blamed him and everyone was understanding and supportive, but he wanted to somehow move past this.

The Delta Protection Detail had been escalating lately and sadly he needed to be ready to fight and protect, possibly to kill again. Papa feared his close friend General Seamons was the leak, but he had no proof of that. The only surviving kidnapper, a Colby Newman, had sworn up and down that he had no idea who'd hired them, and Travis had been the only one to communicate with the man. He didn't think Travis even knew who the man was. He admitted that he thought Flynn did, but of course Flynn was dead so that was no help.

The only good news was whoever had backed the kidnapping and was trying to get to the Delta secret hadn't appeared to share it with anyone else. They didn't have droves of people showing up to find the "treasure". For the past week they'd upped surveillance but nothing out of the ordinary had happened. He could be grateful for that.

Greer turned to walk back to his house. He'd lift weights, eat dinner, read scriptures, listen to some country music, and pray he could sleep tonight.

A movement in the trees caught his gaze. A flash of pink. Pink? That wasn't a natural color in the woods by any means.

He slid his Smith and Wesson .500 pistol out of the holster on his hip and cautiously crept forward. His reaction told him he'd shoot again, if needed. Was that a horrible thing or just instinctive training? He couldn't worry about it right now as there was definitely an intruder moving through the woods toward him. He should inform Papa but he could only see one person. He'd check it out first then pull in the family help if needed.

He reached the edge of the woods and peered in. The person moved around a pine tree and came into full view. She saw him, and stopped in her tracks, her eyes wide and her body visibly trembling.

His breath caught in his chest. A woman. An absolutely gorgeous woman with long, brown curls, a smooth, angelic-looking face, deep-brown eyes, and full lips. Her pink t-shirt was torn and dirty and her gray shorts looked to be the same. Her arms, legs, and even her neck had red scratches and dirt smudges on them.

From running through the woods or had a person done that to her? If anyone hurt her, he would make them regret it. He didn't want to kill again but he was all over pummeling some loser who would hurt an innocent woman.

As they stared at each other he realized he knew this woman.

How? She definitely wasn't from Summit Valley and Greer didn't get out much.

Her gaze darted from his face, across his upper body, and stopped on the gun in his hand. She gasped and backed up, putting her hand over her mouth.

Greer quickly slid the gun back into its holster and held up both hands. "I won't hurt you."

She pulled in quick breaths, her chest rising and falling so quick he hoped she wouldn't hyperventilate. At least she didn't turn around and run, but she looked far from reassured. Did he scare her?

Suddenly it hit him who this beautiful, disheveled woman was. Emery Reeder. That wasn't possible. Was it? He blinked and studied her again. It was her. He could swear it was. The sister of the man he'd killed. What was she doing here? Did she know who Greer was? That might explain the fear in those brown eyes. Greer had the craziest impulse he'd ever had in his life. He wanted to stride to her, pull her into his chest, tell her he was sorry, and hold her until they healed together.

Of course he'd never do something that insane. He stood there. And stared at her. She stared right back. Studied him deeply as if trying to ascertain if he was going to murder her too or maybe if he was friend or foe? If she knew who he was of course she'd hate him. Greer wouldn't blame her, but he wished he could explain he'd reacted instinctively and he couldn't have allowed Alivia or Klein to die. If only he could've placed the shot anywhere besides Travis Reeder's head. Yet if he had, maybe the man would've gotten his own shot off.

The shadows deepened around them and she didn't seem prone to move or say anything. Greer never broke the silence but for some reason he wanted to. He found it was his responsibility to ask, "Are you in danger?"

Her dark eyes flashed at him and for the first time in his life Greer wondered if he was in danger.

"Yes," she squeaked out. She looked over her shoulder as if someone was following her. Greer almost pulled his pistol out again but he didn't want that fear to come back into her eyes.

Suddenly she dodged around some undergrowth and ran at him. Greer stood his ground. He fully expected her to either stick a knife in his gut, punch him, or throw herself into his arms. He prayed hard for the latter, even though he knew that would never be a reality for him and this very surprising woman.

She stopped short of touching him. Dang. Instead she gazed up into his eyes and whispered, "My ex-boyfriend. He tried to ..." She swallowed and didn't finish.

His gut churned. He'd dismantle any man who tried to hurt her. Hadn't she been through enough? Raised in foster care and then losing her only remaining family member. At Greer's hands, but from the way she was looking at him right now he wasn't certain that she had any idea who he was. Had heaven above orchestrated this meeting so Greer could pay penance for killing her brother? He'd have to think on that later. First things first.

He looked over her shoulder. "Is he following you?"

"I don't think so." She shuddered and wrapped her arms around herself. "He brought me to the mountains earlier this afternoon. He told me he just wanted to talk and catch up, but then he tried to force himself on me. I got away. I've been running through the mountains for ... hours."

Greer's eyebrows lifted. That would explain why she looked so disheveled. What he couldn't understand was why it felt like she was telling him a story. Well, maybe he could understand it. If she knew who Greer was she might be making up a story to get close to him, and then she'd plunge a knife through his heart.

"I don't dare go home. He's unstable and dangerous. As I ran he yelled after me that when he finds me he'll kill me."

Greer flinched. Was any of this true? Heck if he knew. Greer wasn't proficient at interpersonal communication. He didn't even talk to his animals.

"He didn't chase you?" If the man wanted to kill her why would he just stand there and let her go? To toy with her? Greer's gaze darted around but he didn't hear or see anything out of the ordinary.

"He ripped his ACL last month playing basketball and luckily he didn't have his gun on him." She shuddered and looked from the gun on Greer's hip then back to his face.

"We should get you to the police," he said.

"Please no. Justin is a policeman."

His eyes widened. "With who?"

"DPD."

Greer swallowed. The Denver Police Department was a lot bigger than Summit Valley's Sheriff's Department and his friend Sheriff Reed. Greer wasn't afraid of anyone and with his family to back him up could take on an army, but he didn't want to force her to go file a statement until she was comfortable. If this was a story he was swallowing it lock, stock, and barrel. Maybe if he had more experience with beautiful women he'd know if she was genuine.

"Please." She looked up at him and he was struck by her beauty and the sweetness in her dark gaze. "Will you protect me?"

"Yes." He nodded solemnly. He'd do anything to make recompense for what he'd done to her. Emery Reeder finding him like this when she was in danger had to be some kind of sign from heaven, possibly an opportunity to make recompense. Every instinct in him was firing to protect this lady from any more harm.

"Can I stay with you until it's safe to go home?"

He studied her. He had plenty of room. If she wasn't Emery

Reeder he'd think heaven had sent a gift, an angel for him to protect and get to know.

Emery Reeder. It was surreal that she was standing right in front of him. He'd been praying for some way to help her. Was this his answer? Greer was supposed to watch over her and somehow help her with her grief? That seemed a bit twisted as he'd caused that grief.

"Yes." He said the word like an oath. He'd keep her safe. But he'd also get ahold of Papa and inform him what was happening. And he'd sleep with his door locked and one eye open.

"Thank you," the words rushed out of her and he'd never loved someone's gratitude so much. "I've been so scared. So alone. You look like a tough, honorable cowboy who will protect me from Justin and anyone else."

Greer didn't know that he'd ever blushed in his life but he could feel his cheeks heating up. He nodded, having no clue what to say to all of that. He was confused.

"What's your name?" she asked softly.

He swallowed. That explained a lot. She had no idea who she'd run to. Once she found out who he was, she might turn and run back to the ex-boyfriend.

"Greer Delta," he said, his gaze not straying from hers.

She didn't even flinch. He blinked in surprise. Did she not know who killed her brother? That actually made sense. The military or police department wouldn't have released the details. Yet somehow he felt like she knew. If she did know she was an extremely impressive actress. Could she be weaseling her way into his life to avenge Travis?

"What's your name?" he asked, figuring he might have to play a part as well until he figured out why she'd really come and if there even was an ex-boyfriend she was running from.

"Taylor Miles."

Greer flinched. So she was going to lie to him. That meant she knew exactly who he was and she was going to set him up.

He guessed there could be another option. Maybe she truly wasn't Emery Reeder. Didn't they claim everybody had a twin out there? She and her brother had obviously had different fathers. If she'd had a promiscuous mother Emery might literally have a twin or sister somewhere in the world. This could be that woman or a woman who looked uncannily like the real Emery Reeder. He had no idea what was truth and what was fiction at this point. All Greer knew was his orderly world was about to get turned upside down.

Keep reading here.

ALSO BY CAMI CHECKETTS

Delta Family Romances

Deceived

Abandoned

Committed

Betrayed

Devoted

Compromised

Endangered

Famous Friends Romances

Loving the Firefighter

Loving the Athlete

Loving the Rancher

Loving the Coach

Loving the Contractor

Loving the Sheriff

Loving the Entertainer

The Hidden Kingdom Romances

Royal Secrets

Royal Security

Royal Doctor

Royal Mistake

Royal Courage

Royal Pilot

Royal Imposter

Royal Baby

Royal Battle

Royal Fake Fiancé

Secret Valley Romance

Sister Pact

Marriage Pact

Christmas Pact

Survive the Romance

Romancing the Treasure

Romancing the Escape

Romancing the Boat

Romancing the Mountain

Romancing the Castle

Romancing the Extreme Adventure

Romancing the Island

Romancing the River

Romancing the Spartan Race

Mystical Lake Resort Romance

Only Her Undercover Spy

Only Her Cowboy

Only Her Best Friend

Only Her Blue-Collar Billionaire

Only Her Injured Stuntman

Only Her Amnesiac Fake Fiancé

Only Her Hockey Legend

Only Her Smokejumper Firefighter

Only Her Christmas Miracle

Jewel Family Romance

Do Marry Your Billionaire Boss

Do Trust Your Special Ops Bodyguard

Do Date Your Handsome Rival

Do Rely on Your Protector

Do Kiss the Superstar

Do Tease the Charming Billionaire

Do Claim the Tempting Athlete

Do Depend on Your Keeper

Strong Family Romance

Don't Date Your Brother's Best Friend

Her Loyal Protector

Don't Fall for a Fugitive

Her Hockey Superstar Fake Fiance

Don't Ditch a Detective

Don't Miss the Moment

Don't Love an Army Ranger

Don't Chase a Player

Don't Abandon the Superstar

Steele Family Romance

Her Dream Date Boss

The Stranded Patriot

The Committed Warrior

Extreme Devotion

Quinn Family Romance

The Devoted Groom

The Conflicted Warrior

The Gentle Patriot

The Tough Warrior

Her Too-Perfect Boss

Her Forbidden Bodyguard

Running Romcom

Running for Love

Taken from Love

Saved by Love

Cami's Collections

Hidden Kingdom Romance Collection

Survive the Romance Collection

Mystical Lake Resort Romance Collection

Billionaire Boss Romance Collection

Jewel Family Collection

The Romance Escape Collection

Cami's Firefighter Collection

Strong Family Romance Collection

Steele Family Collection

Hawk Brothers Collection

Quinn Family Collection

Cami's Georgia Patriots Collection

Cami's Military Collection

Billionaire Beach Romance Collection

Billionaire Bride Pact Collection

Echo Ridge Romance Collection

Texas Titans Romance Collection

Snow Valley Collection

Christmas Romance Collection

Holiday Romance Collection

Extreme Sports Romance Collection

Georgia Patriots Romance

The Loyal Patriot

The Gentle Patriot

The Stranded Patriot

The Pursued Patriot

Jepson Brothers Romance

How to Design Love

How to Switch a Groom

How to Lose a Fiance

Billionaire Boss Romance

Her Dream Date Boss

Her Prince Charming Boss

Hawk Brothers Romance

The Determined Groom

The Stealth Warrior

Her Billionaire Boss Fake Fiance

Risking it All

Navy Seal Romance

The Protective Warrior

The Captivating Warrior

The Stealth Warrior

The Tough Warrior

Texas Titan Romance

The Fearless Groom

The Trustworthy Groom

The Beastly Groom

The Irresistible Groom

The Determined Groom

The Devoted Groom

Billionaire Beach Romance

Caribbean Rescue

Cozumel Escape

Cancun Getaway

Trusting the Billionaire

How to Kiss a Billionaire

Onboard for Love

Shadows in the Curtain

Billionaire Bride Pact Romance

The Resilient One

The Feisty One

The Independent One

The Protective One

The Faithful One

The Daring One

Park City Firefighter Romance

Rescued by Love

Reluctant Rescue

Stone Cold Sparks

Snowed-In for Christmas

Echo Ridge Romance

Christmas Makeover

Last of the Gentlemen

My Best Man's Wedding

Change of Plans

Counterfeit Date

Snow Valley

Full Court Devotion: Christmas in Snow Valley

A Touch of Love: Summer in Snow Valley

Running from the Cowboy: Spring in Snow Valley

Light in Your Eyes: Winter in Snow Valley

Romancing the Singer: Return to Snow Valley

Fighting for Love: Return to Snow Valley

Other Books by Cami

Seeking Mr. Debonair: Jane Austen Pact

Seeking Mr. Dependable: Jane Austen Pact

Saving Sycamore Bay

Oh, Come On, Be Faithful

Protect This

Blog This

Redeem This

The Broken Path

Dead Running

Dying to Run

Fourth of July

Love & Loss

Love & Lies

ABOUT THE AUTHOR

Cami is a part-time author, part-time exercise consultant, part-time housekeeper, full-time wife, and overtime mother of four adorable boys. Sleep and relaxation are fond memories. She's never been happier.

Join Cami's VIP list to find out about special deals, giveaways and new releases and receive a free copy of *Rescued by Love: Park City Firefighter Romance* by clicking here.

cami@camichecketts.com
www.camichecketts.com

Made in United States
Orlando, FL
06 March 2023